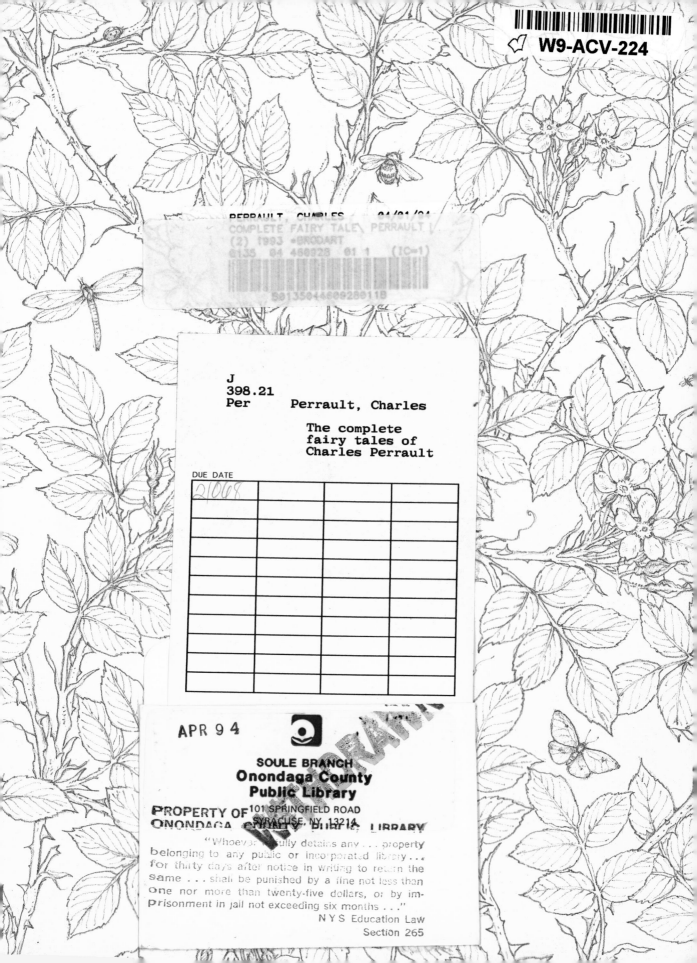

THE COMPLETE
FAIRY TALES
OF
CHARLES PERRAULT

THE COMPLETE
FAIRY TALES
OF
CHARLES PERRAULT

ILLUSTRATED BY
SALLY HOLMES

NEWLY TRANSLATED BY
NEIL PHILIP AND NICOLETTA SIMBOROWSKI

WITH AN INTRODUCTION AND NOTES ON THE STORIES BY
NEIL PHILIP

CLARION BOOKS
NEW YORK

FOR LOUIS AND MAX

Clarion Books
A Houghton Mifflin Company Imprint
215 Park Avenue South, New York, NY 10003

Published in The United States 1993 by arrangement with
The Albion Press Ltd, P.O. Box 52, Princes Risborough,
Bucks HP27 9PR, England

Library of Congress Cataloging-in-Publication Data
Perrault, Charles, 1628-1703.
The Complete Fairy Tales of Charles Perrault/Illustrated by Sally Holmes;
Newly translated by Neil Philip and Nicoletta Simborowski; with an
introduction and notes on the stories by Neil Philip.
P.   CM.
Summary: an illustrated collection of eleven tales including such familiar
titles as ''Cinderella'' and ''The Sleeping Beauty'' and less familiar ones such as
''Tufty Ricky'' and ''The Fairies.''

ISBN 0–395–57002–6

1. Fairy Tales—France—Translations into English. [1. Fairy Tales.
2. Folklore—France.] I. Holmes, Sally, ill. II. Title. PZ8.P426CP 1993
398.21'0944—DC20

92—17781
CIP
AC

Typesetting by York House Typographic, London
Color origination by York House Graphics, London
Printed and bound in Hong Kong by South China Printing Co. (1988) Ltd

10 9 8 7 6 5 4 3 2 1

CONTENTS

INTRODUCTION

"Who wrote Cinderella?" sounds like a trick question. But it has a straightforward answer. "Cinderella" is one of the eight "Tales of Mother Goose" published by Charles Perrault in 1697 which, together with three earlier verse tales, make up the most influential collection of fairy tales before that of the Brothers Grimm, first published in 1812.

Although Perrault did not invent the tales – they are part of the common stock of Indo-European storytelling – he set them in a form that still defines for us what we mean when we say something is "just like a fairy tale." His stories include "Puss-in-Boots," "Little Red Riding Hood," "Bluebeard," and "The Sleeping Beauty" as well as "Cinderella." Each is a classic, and Perrault's wry, detached tellings have formed the basis of almost every subsequent literary version.

Of course, Perrault's writing down the stories did not stop people telling them, as they had always done, by the fireside. I have tried in my notes to each story to place it in the context of the French folktale tradition, and to direct those interested to oral versions collected in France, Great Britain, and the New World.

The stories were old, but what Perrault did with them was new. Writing for a jaded audience at the sumptuous court of Louis XIV of France, he entertained them with the simple stories of the people. He gave the tales a more courtly dress and a more knowing air than they would have had in a peasant's cottage, but he did not make fun of them or spoil them with literary embroidery. He let them speak for themselves, and in the process revealed that what they had to say was not so simple after all.

Iona and Peter Opie wrote in *The Classic Fairy Tales*:

> Perrault's achievement was that he accepted the fairy tales at their own level. He recounted them without impatience, without mockery, and without feeling they required any aggrandisement, such as a frame-story, though he did end each tale with a rhymed *moralité*. If only it had occurred to him to state where he had obtained each tale, and under what circumstances, he would probably today be revered as the father of folklore.

But if folklore as a science did not exist in Perrault's day, storytelling as an art did, and he showed a remarkable understanding of the inner workings of the fairy tale and of the logic by which its magic works.

The fairy tale could be defined as a story in which the characters, by means of a series of transformations, discover their true selves. Much wisdom is encoded in such tales, which are, suggests modern master storyteller Duncan Williamson, "telling us how to live in this world as natural human beings." The inner meaning of such stories cannot easily be explained or defined. Rather, they are full of possible meanings, which resonate with the experiences and the characters of teller and listener.

12

It was when Charles Perrault realized that he did not have to put such tales into verse, for they were already a form of poetry, that he discovered how to take the spoken tale and set it imperishably on the printed page. Folklorists who came later, such as Emmanuel Cosquin, Paul Sébillot, François-Marie Luzel, Paul Delarue, and Geneviève Massignon, were to harvest the folktales of France in the very words of their tellers, recording with dedication and scrupulous scholarship the riches of French folk tradition. But Perrault, writing a century before the study of folklore had ever been thought of, was the first to value such stories for themselves. His versions remain some of the most popular and the most powerful of all.

This new translation of Perrault's eleven stories aims to do justice to his achievement, and to retain the sharpness of wit that is much more characteristic of him than the sloppy sentimentality of so many retellings. Perrault's astringency sets him apart from the other French writers of his day who followed the new fashion for fairy tales. They have been forgotten; he has become immortal.

NEIL PHILIP
PRINCES RISBOROUGH
1992

THE SLEEPING BEAUTY

THERE WERE ONCE a king and queen who were very upset that they had no children at all, more upset than words can say. They went all over the world taking the waters, making vows and pilgrimages, and performing every devotion. They tried everything and nothing seemed to work. At last, however, the queen became pregnant and gave birth to a daughter. The king and queen had scoured the land for seven fairies to stand as godmothers for the little princess, and each gave her a gift as was the custom with fairies in those days. In this way, the princess could acquire every perfection.

They held a fine christening, and after the ceremony the whole party went back to the king's palace, where a great feast had been prepared for the fairies. Before each one was laid a magnificent place setting, with a thick gold casket containing a knife, fork, and spoon of fine gold, decorated with diamonds and rubies. But, as each took her place at table, an old fairy was seen coming in. No one had invited her because she had been shut up in her tower for more than fifty years and everyone thought she was dead or else spellbound.

15

The king ordered a place to be set for her, but he was unable to give her a thick golden casket like the others, because he had had only seven made, for the seven fairy god-mothers.

The old fairy thought they were insulting her and muttered a few threats through gritted teeth. One of the younger fairies, who was seated near her, heard her and, realizing that she might well give some unpleasant gift to the little princess, slipped from the table and hid behind the tapestry, so that she could speak last and do her best to repair any damage that the old fairy might do.

Next the fairies began to give their gifts to the princess. The youngest gave her as a gift that she would be the most beautiful person in the world, the next that she would have the wit of an angel, the third that she would move with enchanting grace, the fourth that she would dance to perfection, the fifth that she would sing like a nightingale, and the sixth that she would play every musical instrument. The old fairy's turn came, and, her head shaking even more from spite than from age, she said that the princess would prick her finger with a spindle, and die.

This terrible gift made the whole gathering tremble, and there was not one person who did not weep. At that moment, the young fairy stepped out from behind the tapestry and declared, "Take comfort, king and queen, your daughter will not die. It is true that I have not enough power to undo entirely what my elder has done. The princess will prick her finger with a spindle, but instead of dying she will merely fall into a deep sleep that will last a hundred years, at the end of which a king's son will come and wake her."

In spite of this, the king did his best to avert the old fairy's curse by publishing an edict forbidding anyone to use a spinning wheel or to keep spindles in the house, on pain of death.

Fifteen or sixteen years later, the king and queen were spending the summer at a castle in the country. Exploring the castle one day, the young princess climbed from room to room, right to the top of a tower, to a little garret where an old lady sat alone, spinning her wheel. This good lady had not heard anything at all about the king's ruling against using a spindle.

"What are you doing, my good woman?" asked the princess.

"I'm spinning, my pretty dear," replied the old lady, who did not recognize her.

"Oh! What fun!" continued the princess. "How do you do that? Let me try."

As she worked swiftly and a little heedlessly, and as, besides, the fairy decree had ordered it so, she had no sooner taken hold of the spindle than she pricked her finger with it and fell down in a faint.

The old lady, in a great state, cried out for help. People came running from all sides. They threw water in the princess's face and unlaced her stays, they chafed her hands, they rubbed her temples with eau-de-cologne; but nothing brought her back to life.

The king, who had come up to find out what the noise was about, remembered the fairy's curse. What must be, must be, especially if the fairies say so. So the king had the princess taken to the most beautiful suite of rooms in the palace and laid on a bed embroidered with gold and silver. You would have thought she was an angel, she was so beautiful; the trance had not taken away the brightness of her complexion. Her cheeks were still rosy and her lips like coral. Her eyes were closed, but you could hear her breathing softly, which showed that she was not dead. The king ordered that she should be allowed to sleep in peace until the hour of her awakening came.

The good fairy, who had saved her life by condemning her to sleep for a hundred years, was in the kingdom of Mataquin, twelve thousand leagues away, when the accident befell the princess. But she soon heard the news from a little dwarf who had seven-league boots, which cover seven leagues in a single stride. The fairy started out immediately and an hour later could be seen arriving in a chariot of fire drawn by dragons. The king went to offer her his hand as she got out of the chariot. She approved of all he had done; but as she had great foresight, she felt that when the princess awoke she would feel very ill at ease all alone in that old castle, so this is what she did. She touched with her wand everything that was in the castle apart from the king and queen: the housekeepers, the ladies-in-waiting, the chambermaids, the gentlemen, the officers, the butlers, the cooks, the kitchen boys, the errand boys, the guards, the soldiers, the pages, the footmen. She also touched the horses in the stables, with their grooms, the great watchdogs in the yard, and even the princess's little pet cat, which was next to her on the bed.

As soon as she touched all these, they fell asleep and would not wake again until their mistress did, so that they would be there ready to serve her when she needed them. Even the spits over the fire, laden with partridges and pheasants, slumbered, and the fire slept too. All this was done in a moment; fairies are not slow at their work.

So, having kissed their dear child without waking her, the king and queen left the castle and published edicts forbidding anyone to approach it. These edicts, however, proved to be unnecessary, as within a quarter of an hour there grew all around the castle grounds such a huge quantity of trees and bushes, of brambles and thorns, all enmeshed with one another, that neither man nor beast could get through; you could not even see the top of the castle turrets, unless you were very far away. That was how the fairy kept the sleeping princess safe from prying eyes.

After a hundred years, the son of the king reigning at that time, who was from a different family than that of the sleeping princess, had gone hunting in those parts. He asked what the turrets were that he could see above a huge, thick wood, and everyone replied according to what he had heard. Some said that it was an old castle, haunted by ghosts; others that it was where all the witches in the land held their sabbath. The most popular story was that an ogre lived there and took back to the castle all the children he caught, to eat them at his leisure without anyone following him, since only he was strong enough to make his way through the wood.

The prince did not know what to believe. Then an old farmer spoke, saying, "My prince, more than fifty years ago I heard someone tell my father that the most beautiful princess in the world was asleep in that castle, and that she would sleep for a hundred years, until a king's son came to wake her and claim her."

The young prince was instantly inflamed with passion by these words. Here was a wonderful adventure, and he determined at once to pursue it to the end. Fired by thoughts of love and glory, he resolved to find out the secret of the wood.

As soon as he entered the wood all those great trees, and the interlaced brambles and thorns, separated to let him pass. He walked toward the castle, which he could see at the end of a great avenue. He was surprised that none of his companions had been able to follow him, since the trees had closed in again as soon as he had passed. But he did not falter; a young prince in love is always brave.

He entered the castle and found himself in a great courtyard, where all that he set eyes on was enough to freeze him with terror. There was a dreadful silence, and the image of death was everywhere. The bodies of men and animals lay scattered on the ground, apparently lifeless. However, he soon realized from the glowing noses and ruddy faces of the guards that they were merely sleeping, and the dregs of wine in their glasses showed that they had been drinking when they dozed off.

He went through another marble courtyard and climbed the stairs to the guardroom. The guards were standing in line, rifles on their shoulders, snoring fit to burst. He went through several rooms full of gentlemen and ladies, some standing, some seated, all asleep. Then he went into a room of gold and saw on the bed, whose curtains were open on all sides, the most beautiful sight he had ever seen.

On the bed was a princess, a young girl of fifteen or sixteen, whose untarnished beauty seemed to shine with an unearthly radiance. He approached in trembling admiration and fell on his knees before her. And so, as the spell had now been broken, the princess woke. Looking at him with eyes so tender and loving

that you would never believe he was a stranger, she said, "Is it really you, my prince? You certainly took your time."

Charmed by these words and even more so by the tone in which they were uttered, the prince did not know how to show her his joy and gratitude. He told her that he loved her more than he loved himself. His words were garbled, but that made them all the more pleasing: not much eloquence, but lots of love. He was more embarrassed than she was, and really one shouldn't be surprised, for she had had plenty of time to dream about what she was going to say to him; the good fairy had beguiled her long sleep with such sweet dreams.

In all, they talked to each other for four hours and still had not said even half of the things they wanted to say to each other.

Meanwhile, the whole palace had woken up with the princess. Each person set about his work, and since they weren't all in love, they were starving. The lady-in-waiting, as peckish as the others, began to get impatient and said loudly to the princess that the meat was ready.

The prince helped the princess to get up. She was fully dressed in magnificent style, but he was very careful not to tell her that she was dressed like his grandmother, because she was no less beautiful for being out of fashion.

They dined in a room of mirrors, waited on by the princess's servants and listening to her musicians play the old violins and oboes which still sounded true, even though no one had played them for a hundred years.

After supper, without wasting any more time, the chaplain married them in the castle chapel and the lady-in-waiting drew the curtains round their bed.

They didn't get much sleep; the princess didn't feel drowsy, and the prince left her at daybreak to go back to the town, where his father was bound to be worrying about him.

The prince told his father that he had got lost in the forest while hunting and that he had slept in a charcoal-burner's hut and had been given black bread and cheese to eat. The king, his father, was easygoing and believed him, but his mother was not so easily fooled. When she saw that he was going hunting almost every day and that he always had some excuse at the ready when he had spent two or three nights out, she soon guessed that he had some romantic entanglement.

He lived with the princess for almost two whole years and had two children by her. The first was a daughter, called Dawn, and the second a son, whom they called Day, because he looked even more beautiful than his sister.

Hoping to make him explain himself, the queen several times told her son that he should settle down, but he never dared tell her his secret. For though he loved her, he feared her, as she was descended from ogres and the king had only married her for her money. It was even whispered at court that she had inherited the appetites of ogres and that when she saw little children passing by, she could barely keep herself from falling upon them. So the prince did not want to tell her ever. But when the king died two years later, and he became king himself, he declared his marriage publicly and went with great ceremony to collect his wife the queen and bring her back to his castle. Cheering crowds welcomed her to the town, with her children on either side.

Some time later, the king went off to wage war against the Emperor Cantalabutte. He left his mother in charge of the kingdom and begged her to look after his wife and children. He was to be away at war for the whole summer.

As soon as he had gone, the queen mother sent her daughter-in-law and the children to the country, to a house deep in the woods, so that she could satisfy her horrible appetites with greater ease. She followed them a few days later and said one evening to her chef, "Tomorrow I wish to have little Dawn for my dinner."

"Oh, my lady!" said the chef.

"That's what I want," said the queen, and she said it in the tone of an ogress who has a fancy for fresh flesh. "Serve her with a piquant sauce."

The poor man, realizing that it was folly to mess with an ogress, took his carving knife and went up to little Dawn's room. She was then four years old and came dashing up to him, threw her arms round his neck with a laugh, and asked him for treats.

He began to cry, the knife fell from his hands, and he went down into the yard and cut a lamb's throat. He prepared it with such a tasty sauce that his mistress assured him she had never eaten anything so good. Meanwhile, he had spirited little Dawn away and entrusted her to his wife to hide in her lodgings in the lower courtyard.

Eight days later, the wicked queen said to her chef, "I want little Day for my supper."

He did not reply, determined to trick her as before. He went to look for little Day and found him with a tiny sword in his hand, battling with a huge monkey, and he was only three. He took him to his wife and she hid him with little Dawn, and in his place he cooked a very tender kid goat for the ogress, and she smacked her lips at every mouthful.

All had gone very well up to that point, but one evening the wicked queen said to the chef, "I want to eat the queen in the same sauce as I had her children."

That was when the poor chef despaired of being able to deceive her again. The young queen was past twenty, not to mention the hundred years she had slept, and her flesh was rather tough, however beautiful and white. He was unlikely to find a creature in the farmyard as tough as that; in order to save his own life, he resolved to cut the queen's throat. He went up to her room, determined to get it over with. He worked himself up into a fury, then went into the young queen's chamber, his dagger in his hand. However, he did not want to take her by surprise, and told her very respectfully what the queen mother had ordered him to do.

"Do what you must," she said, offering him her throat. "Carry out the order you have been given. I will see my children again, my poor children that I loved so much." For she thought they were dead, since they had been taken and she had been told nothing.

The poor chef's heart melted. "No, no, my lady," he said. "You don't need to die to see your children again. Come to my home, where I have hidden them. I will deceive the queen again, by giving her a young deer to eat in your place." He took her to his rooms straightaway and left her to kiss her children and weep with them. He went off to get hold of a deer, which the queen mother dined on with the same relish as if it had been the young queen. She gloated over her cruelty, and enjoyed thinking how she would tell the king on his return that wild wolves had eaten the queen and her two children.

One evening, she was roaming as usual around the yards and courtyards of the palace, sniffing for fresh meat, when she heard coming from a cellar the sound of Day crying. His mother the queen wanted to beat him, as he had been naughty. She also heard little Dawn begging pardon on behalf of her brother. The ogress recognized the queen's voice and her children's voices. Furious at having been tricked, she commanded in a terrible voice, which made everyone tremble, that the following morning a huge vat should be brought into the courtyard, filled with toads, vipers, snakes, and serpents, and into it should be thrown the queen, her children, the chef, his wife, and his serving girl.

She had given the order for them to be brought forward, their hands tied behind their backs. They were there, and the executioners were preparing to throw them into the vat, when the king, who was not expected back so soon, rode into the courtyard. He had come in haste and asked, astonished, what this horrible spectacle meant. Nobody dared tell him, and the ogress, in a rage of frustration, herself dived headfirst into the vat and was devoured in an instant by the foul creatures within.

The king couldn't help grieving, for she was his mother, after all, but he soon consoled himself with his lovely wife and children.

MORAL

This story will allay your fears
If Love's a waiting game for you;
But to sleep away a hundred years
Is too much to expect a girl to do.

For Sleeping Beauty there was nothing lost
By waiting before getting hitched;
A girl can dally without counting cost
For a groom who's handsome, kind, and rich.

But truth to tell, young girls are ardent;
They long for their own prince to come:
And I am not yet quite so hardened
As to press this moral home.

LITTLE RED RIDING HOOD

THERE WAS ONCE a little village girl, the prettiest you
ever saw. Her mother doted on her and her grandmother
even more so. This good lady had a little red cloak made
for her, which suited her so well that everyone called her Little
Red Riding Hood.

One day her mother made some bread and said to her, "Go
and see how your grandmother is, for I hear she's been ill. Take
her a loaf and this little pot of butter."

Little Red Riding Hood left straightaway to go and visit her
grandmother, who lived in another village. On her way
through the wood, she met a wolf, who quite fancied eating her
but did not dare, because of the woodcutters who were working
in the forest.

He asked her where she was going. The poor child, who did
not know that it is dangerous to stop and chat with wolves, said
to him, "I'm going to see my grandmother, to take her a loaf
with a little pot of butter that my mother has sent."

"Does she live very far away?" asked the wolf.

"Oh, yes," said Little Red Riding Hood. "It's beyond that mill

you can see over there.
Right there, the first
house in the village.''

''Well,'' said the wolf, ''I
want to go and see her too. I'll
go by this road and you by that
one, and we'll see who gets
there first.''

The wolf started to run as
fast as he could by the shortcut, and the little girl took
the longer path, dawdling to
pick some hazelnuts,
chase after butterflies,
and make little bunches
of the wayside flowers.

The wolf soon arrived at the
grandmother's house. He knocked:
Rat! Tat!

''Who's there?''

''It's your granddaughter, Little Red Riding
Hood,'' said the wolf, disguising his voice. ''I've brought
you a loaf and a little pot of butter that my mother has sent
you.''

The kindly grandmother, who was in bed as she wasn't well,
called out to him, ''Pull the handle, the latch will give.'' The
wolf pulled the handle and the door opened.

He flung himself on the good woman and gobbled her up, for
it was more than three days since he had eaten. Then he closed
the door and tucked himself up in the grandmother's bed to

31

wait for Little Red Riding Hood, who, shortly afterward, came and knocked at the door: Rat! Tat!

"Who's there?"

When Little Red Riding Hood heard the wolf's hoarse voice, she was afraid at first, but, thinking that her grandmother must have a cold, she replied, "It's your granddaughter, Little Red Riding Hood. I've brought you a loaf and a little pot of butter that my mother has sent you."

The wolf called out, softening his voice a little, "Pull the handle, the latch will give." Little Red Riding Hood pulled the handle and the door opened. When the wolf saw her come in, he hid under the blankets and said, "Put the loaf and the little pot of butter in the bread bin and come and get into bed with me."

Little Red Riding Hood got undressed and climbed into bed, where she was most surprised to see what her grandmother was like with nothing on.

She said, "Grandmother! What big arms you have!"

"All the better to hug you with, my dear!"

"Grandmother! What big legs you have!"

"All the better to chase you with, my dear!"

"Grandmother! What big ears you have!"

"All the better to hear you with, my dear!"

"Grandmother! What big eyes you have!"

"All the better to see you with, my dear!"

"Grandmother! What big teeth you have!"

"All the better to eat you with!"

And with these words, that wicked wolf leapt upon Little Red Riding Hood and ate her.

MORAL

Young children, as we clearly see,
Pretty girls, especially,
Innocent of all life's dangers,
Shouldn't stop and chat with strangers.
If this simple advice beats them,
It's no surprise if a wolf eats them.

And this warning take, I beg:
Not every wolf runs on four legs.
The smooth tongue of a smooth-skinned creature
May mask a rough and wolfish nature.
These quiet types, for all their charm,
Can be the cause of the worse harm.

BLUEBEARD

THERE WAS ONCE a man who owned grand houses in the town and country, gold and silver dinnerware, tapestries and gilded carriages. But, sadly, he also had a blue beard. This made him so ugly and frightening that women and girls fled at the sight of him.

A high-class lady who lived nearby had two perfectly beautiful daughters. He asked her for the hand of one of them in marriage and left to her the choice of which one it should be. Neither of them wanted him at all and each fobbed him off onto the other, unable to resign themselves to the idea of marrying a man with a blue beard. What repelled them even more was that he had already married several times, and no one knew what had become of these women.

In order to get to know them, Bluebeard invited the girls with their mother, three or four of their best friends, and a few young people from the area, to one of his houses in the country, where they stayed for eight whole days. All they did was hold picnics and parties. They hunted and fished, danced and ate, and no one slept a wink; they were too busy playing the fool. In fact, all went so well that the younger sister stopped worrying about the lord of the manor's blue beard and decided that he was a fine man after all. As soon as they got back to the town, she married him.

After a month, Bluebeard told his wife that he had to make a trip into the provinces on important business and would be away for at least six weeks. He told her to amuse herself during his absence. If she liked, she could invite all her friends and take them to the country; anything that would keep her happy.

He handed her a great bunch of keys. "These are for the two large storerooms," he said, "and these are for the strongboxes where I keep gold and silver dinnerware that we don't use every day. These are for my coffers of gold and silver, these are for the jewel safes, and here is the master key for all the rooms in the house. But this little key here is the key to the room at the end of the great gallery on the ground floor; open everything, go everywhere, but I forbid you to enter that little room. If you disobey me in this, nothing will protect you from my anger."

She promised to do as he told her. He kissed her, climbed into his carriage, and set off on his journey.

The young bride's friends couldn't wait to be asked to visit, they were so impatient to see the riches in the house, not having dared to come there while her husband was home as they were afraid of his blue beard. They lost no time in exploring the rooms, each lovelier and richer than the one before. Then they went up to the storerooms, where they gasped at the profusion of beautiful tapestries, beds, sofas, cabinets, and tables. There were mirrors in which you could see yourself from head to foot and whose frames, some of reflecting glass, the others of silver and gilt, were the finest they had ever seen. They were bowled over by the good fortune of their friend. Only she was not really enjoying herself, because all the time she was dying to open the door to the forbidden room. She was so consumed with curiosity that without considering how rude it was to leave her guests, she ran downstairs by a small, hidden staircase at such a gallop that two or three times she thought she was going to break her neck.

When she arrived at the door of the room, she stopped for a moment, remembering how firmly her husband had spoken and thinking that he might punish her for being disobedient; but the temptation was too strong for her to resist. So she took the little key and, trembling, opened the door of the room.

At first she couldn't see anything because the shutters were closed. After a few moments she began to see that the floor was sticky with clotted blood; worse, she could see reflected in this blood the corpses of several women, hanging up along the walls. These were all the women that Bluebeard had married and whose throats he had cut, one after the other.

She thought she would die of fear, and the key of the room, which she had just drawn out of its lock, fell from her hand. When she had pulled herself together a little, she picked up the key, relocked the door, and went up to her bedroom to recover, but she was so distressed that she fainted on the way.

She noticed that the key was stained with blood, and so she wiped it two or three times, but the blood would not go away. Washing it was no use, and scrubbing it with sand and grease was no better; the blood was still there, for the key was enchanted and there was no way of cleaning it. When the blood was removed from one side it reappeared on the other.

Bluebeard came back from his trip that same evening and said he had received letters on the way telling him that the business which had called him away had been settled already. His wife did all she could to show him she was delighted by his prompt return.

The following day he asked for his keys back and she gave them to him. Her hand was shaking so badly that he easily guessed what had happened.

"How come the key to the little room is not here with the others?" he asked.

"I must have left it upstairs on my table," she said.

"I need the key now," said Bluebeard. There was no use in delay; she had to give him the key. Bluebeard looked at it, then said to his wife, "Why is there blood on this key?"

"I don't know anything about it," replied the poor woman, paler than death.

"You don't know anything about it," repeated Bluebeard. "Well, I know. So you couldn't resist going into that room? Well then, madam, you will go in there, and you will take your place beside the ladies you saw there."

She flung herself at her husband's feet, crying and begging forgiveness, with every sign of being truly sorry for her disobedience. She would have wrung pity from a stone in her beauty and distress, but Bluebeard's heart was harder than stone.

"Madam, you must die," he told her. "Your hour has come."

"Since I must die," she replied, looking at him, her eyes filled with tears, "give me a little time to say my prayers."

"I will give you a quarter of an hour," said Bluebeard, "but not a moment longer."

When she was alone, she called her sister Anne and said, "Anne, I beg you, go to the top of the tower and see if our brothers are coming. They promised me they would come to see me today, and if you see them, signal to them to hurry.'' Her sister Anne climbed to the top of the tower, and the poor unfortunate wife called to her from time to time, "Anne, my sister Anne, don't you see anything coming?''

And her sister Anne would reply, "I see nothing but the dust made gold by the sun and the green of the grass.''

Meanwhile, Bluebeard, holding a huge cutlass in his hand, was shouting up at his wife as loud as he could, "Come down quickly or I'll come up there!''

"Just one more minute!'' replied his wife and immediately called out quietly, "Anne, my sister Anne, don't you see anything coming?''

And her sister Anne replied, "I see nothing but the dust shining gold in the sun, and the green grass growing.''

"Come down quickly or I'll come up there!'' shouted Bluebeard.

"I'm coming,'' replied his wife, then called, "Anne, my sister Anne, don't you see anything coming?''

"I can see a huge cloud of dust in the distance,'' replied her sister Anne.

"Is it my brothers?''

"Alas no, my sister, it's a flock of sheep.''

"Are you coming down or not?'' shouted Bluebeard.

"Just a minute more!'' replied his wife and then called, "Anne, my sister Anne, don't you see anything coming?''

"I can see two riders approaching,'' she replied, "but they are still a long way off.'' And then, "God be praised! It is our brothers. Oh, hurry! Hurry!''

Bluebeard began to shout so loud that the whole house

trembled. His poor wife went down and threw herself in disarray at his feet, sobbing.

"That will do you no good," said Bluebeard, "you must die." Then, taking her by the hair with one hand, he raised the cutlass in the other, ready to cut off her head. The poor woman turned toward him and, gazing at him with dimmed eyes, begged him to give her a moment to collect herself.

"No, no," he said, "commend your soul to God." And, raising his arm — At that moment there was such a loud knock at the door that Bluebeard stopped in his tracks. The door was opened and two horse-men came in, naked swords in their hands, and rushed

straight at Bluebeard. He recognized them as his wife's brothers, one a dragoon, the other a musketeer, and so he fled, but the two brothers were so close behind that they caught him before he had time to reach the staircase. They ran him through with their swords and left him dead.

42

The poor wife lay on the floor, almost as lifeless as her husband, without even the strength to rise and kiss her brothers.

Bluebeard left no heirs, and so his wife became mistress of all his belongings. She used some of the money to marry her sister Anne to a young gentleman who had loved her for a long time; she used another sum to buy a captain's commission for each of her brothers, and the rest she used to marry herself to a good man, who helped her forget the terrible time she had spent with Bluebeard.

MORAL

Curiosity has its lure,
But all the same
It's a paltry kind of pleasure
And a risky game.
The thrill of peeping is soon over;
And then the cost is to discover.

ANOTHER MORAL

Anyone with half an eye
Can see this tale's of times gone by.
No husband wants his wife to cower,
Or thinks that she is in his power.
Once the wife's made up her mind,
The husband meekly trails behind.
If you see a man and wife at large,
No need to guess just who's in charge.

PUSS-IN-BOOTS

A MILLER DIED, and all he left to his three sons was his mill, his ass, and his cat. The goods were shared out without the assistance of a notary or a lawyer of any kind, who would soon have swallowed up the tiny inheritance. The eldest son had the mill, the second the ass, and the youngest just the cat. He felt very ill used.

He said, "My brothers will be able to join together to earn an honest living. But as for me, once I've eaten my cat and made myself a muff out of his pelt, I'll just have to starve."

The cat, who had been listening to this but pretending not to, said in a calm, serious voice, "Do not despair, master. All you have to do is give me a sack and have a pair of boots made for me for walking through the brambles, and you will see that you have not done so badly from the share-out after all."

Although the cat's master did not set any great store by what the cat said, he had seen this cat perform some amazing acrobatic feats in order to catch rats and mice, as for example when he hung from his feet or hid in the flour and played dead,

and so he was quite hopeful
that the cat could help him
in his dire straits.

When the cat had what he had
asked for, he put on his boots with a
flourish, put the sack round his neck,
holding the drawstrings with his two front
paws, and went off to a warren where there
was a large number of rabbits. He put some
bran and some green stuff in his sack and,
stretching out as if dead, waited for some innocent young rabbit to come and forage in his sack
and eat what he had put there. He had scarcely lain
down when he had success. A silly bunny went
into his sack and Puss immediately pulled the
cords tight, caught the rabbit, and killed it without
mercy.

Proudly bearing his catch, he went off to the king
and asked to speak to him. He was taken up to his majesty's
rooms. He went in, bowed low to the king, and said, "Sire, I
have here a wild rabbit which my master, his excellency the
Marquis of Carabas (for that was the name he had invented for
the miller's son), has ordered me to present to you on his
behalf."

"Tell your master," replied the king, "that I thank him for his
gracious gift."

On another occasion, the cat went and hid in the corn, his
sack open as before. When two partridges went in, he pulled the
cords tight and caught them both. He went and presented them
to the king straightaway, as he had done with the wild rabbit.

The king
accepted
the two
partridges
with pleasure
and offered the
cat something to
drink.

The cat continued in this way for two or three months, from time to time taking the king game from his master's hunting. One day, when he knew that the king was going to take a ride along the riverside with his daughter, the most beautiful princess in the world, he said to his master, "If you follow my advice, your fortune is made. All you have to do is go and bathe in the river in the place I will show you and then leave everything to me."

The Marquis of Carabas did what his cat advised him,

without knowing what good it would do. While he was bathing, the king passed by, and the cat started shouting out at the top of his voice, "Help! Help! The Marquis of Carabas is drowning!"

When the king heard this cry, he put his head out through the carriage door, and recognizing the cat who had brought him game so many times, he ordered his guards to hurry and help the Marquis of Carabas. As the poor marquis was being pulled from the river, the cat went up to the carriage and told the king that while the marquis was bathing, some thieves had come and stolen his clothes, even though he had cried "Stop thief!" as loud as he could. Cunning Puss had hidden his master's rags under a large rock.

The king immediately ordered his officers of the wardrobe to go and fetch one of his finest robes for his excellency the Marquis of Carabas. The king greeted the marquis with many compliments, and as the beautiful clothes the young man had just been given set off his attractive looks (for he was handsome and well built), the king's daughter too found him greatly to her liking. The Marquis of Carabas only had to send two or three tender but respectful glances in her direction and she was madly in love with him.

The king wanted him to get into the carriage and ride with them. The cat, delighted to see that his plan was beginning to succeed, went on ahead, and when he met some peasants cutting hay in a field, he said, "Good folk, if you do not tell the king that the field in which you are cutting hay belongs to his excellency the Marquis of Carabas, you will all be hacked up into mincemeat."

The king did not fail to ask the workers who owned the field they were mowing.

"It belongs to his excellency the Marquis of Carabas," they all said together, for the cat's threat had frightened them.

"You have a fine inheritance there," said the king to the Marquis of Carabas.

"As you see, sire," replied the marquis, "that field never fails to bring in a rich harvest every year."

Master Puss, who was still ahead, met some harvesters and said, "Good folk, if you do not tell the king that all this corn belongs to his excellency the Marquis of Carabas, you will all be hacked up into mincemeat."

The king, who passed by a moment later, wanted to know who owned all the corn he could see.

"It belongs to his excellency the Marquis of Carabas," replied the harvesters, and the king congratulated the marquis again.

The cat continued to go on ahead of the carriage and to say the same thing to everyone he met. The king was astonished by how much the Marquis of Carabas owned.

Master Puss finally reached a beautiful castle that belonged to an ogre, the richest anyone had ever known, for in fact all the lands the king had passed through were part of this castle's estate.

The cat had taken good care to find out who this ogre was and what his powers were. Puss asked to see him, saying that he had not wanted to pass so near his castle without paying his respects. The ogre received him as politely as an ogre can and had him sit down.

"I've been assured," said the cat, "that you have the gift of being able to change into all kinds of animals — that you can, for example, change into a lion or an elephant."

"That's true," snapped back the ogre, "and to prove it to you,

you'll see me turn into a lion." The cat was so terrified to see a lion before him that he jumped right up to the roof, where he could barely cling on, owing to the boots he was wearing, which were useless for walking on tiles.

A little later, seeing that the ogre had changed back again, the cat came down and admitted that he had been pretty frightened.

"I've also been assured," said the cat, "though I really can't believe it, that you have the power to change yourself into the smallest of creatures, for example a rat or a mouse. I have to tell you that I consider that quite impossible."

"Impossible?" said the ogre. "You'll see." And as he spoke he changed into a mouse, which began to run about on the floor. In a trice, the cat leapt on it and ate it.

Meanwhile, the king had seen the lovely castle as he passed by and wanted to go in. The cat heard the sound of the carriage coming over the drawbridge, ran to meet it, and said to the king, "Welcome, your majesty, to the castle of his excellency the Marquis of Carabas."

"Well, well, your excellency," cried the king, "so this castle is yours too! There can be nothing more beautiful than this courtyard and all the buildings around it. Let us see the interior, if you please."

The marquis held out his hand to the young princess and, following the king, who went in first, they entered a great hall. There they found a magnificent supper which the ogre had had prepared for his friends, who were supposed to have come that same day to see him but had not dared come in, knowing that the king was there.

The king was just as charmed by his excellency the Marquis

of Carabas as his daughter, who was mad about him; besides his other fine qualities, he owned so much property! So after five or six drinks, the king said, "It is your decision, your excellency, whether you are to be my son-in-law."

The marquis bowed low and accepted with pleasure; he and the princess were married that very day. As for master Puss, he became a great lord and didn't chase mice anymore except to amuse himself.

MORAL

It's all very well to be born rich,
And pass on wealth from father to son;
But hard work, know-how, and quick wits
Are just as useful, when you're young.

ANOTHER MORAL

You ask how a mere miller's son
Could win the heart of a true princess?
That's because love is easily won
By a poor boy in a rich one's dress.

THE FAIRIES

THERE WAS ONCE a widow who had two daughters. The elder was the spitting image of her mother, in character and looks. Both were so disagreeable and conceited that they were impossible to live with. The younger, who was the image of her father in her gentleness and courtesy, was also one of the most beautiful girls you ever did see. As we all naturally love those like ourselves, this mother adored her elder daughter and at the same time loathed the younger one. She made her eat in the kitchen and slave from morning to night.

One of the poor child's chores was to go twice a day to a spring a good half-league from their house and bring back a large pitcher full of water. One day she was at the spring when a poor woman came up to her and begged her for a drink.

"Of course, dear lady," said this lovely girl and immediately rinsed out her pitcher, filled it where the spring water flowed most purely, and held it out to her, holding the pitcher carefully so that she could drink more easily.

The old woman was really a fairy who had taken the shape of

a poor village woman just to test the girl's good heart. So when she had finished her drink she said to the girl, "You are so beautiful, so good, and so kind that I must give you something in return. My gift is this: For every word you say, either a flower or a precious stone will drop from your mouth."

When the pretty girl got home, her mother scolded her for dawdling on the way.

"I'm sorry," said the poor girl, "for taking so long." As she spoke, out of her mouth came two roses, two pearls, and two large diamonds.

"What's that I see?" said her mother in astonishment. "I do believe pearls and diamonds are coming out of her mouth. Where do they come from, daughter?"

That was the first time she had ever called her "daughter." The poor child innocently told her all that happened, scattering countless diamonds as she spoke.

"Really?" said the mother. "Well, I must send my daughter. Look, Fanchon, look what comes out of your sister's mouth when she speaks. Wouldn't you like to have the same gift? All you have to do is go and fetch water at the spring, and when a poor woman asks you for water, give it to her kindly."

"You'll not catch me fetching water at the spring," Fanchon replied roughly.

"I want you to go," answered her mother, "this minute." So she went, grumbling, on her way. Instead of a clay pitcher, she took the best silver flask they had in the house.

No sooner had she arrived at the spring than a magnificently dressed lady came out of the wood, approached her, and asked her for a drink. This was the same fairy who had appeared to her sister, but had taken on the clothing and appearance of a princess in order to see just how far this girl's ill nature would go.

"I suppose I've come here just to wait on you, have I?" said the rude, arrogant girl. "Oh, yes, I've lugged a silver flask all this way specially to serve madam her drink. Well, you can drink from the spring, for all I care."

"You are hardly kindhearted," said the fairy, without getting angry. "Well, since you are so unhelpful, I'll give you the gift that at every word you say either a serpent or a toad will spit out of your mouth."

As soon as her mother spotted her, she shouted, "Well, daughter?"

"Not so well, mother," replied the slattern, spitting out two vipers and two toads.

"Oh Lord!" cried the mother. "What's that I see? This is your sister's fault! I'll make her pay for this." And off she ran to beat her. The poor child fled and took refuge in the forest nearby.

The king's son, who was returning from the hunt, chanced upon her and, noticing how beautiful she was, asked her what she was doing all alone and why she was crying.

"Alas, sir! My mother has thrown me out of the house." The king's son saw five or six pearls and as many diamonds tumbling from her mouth and asked her where they came from. She told him the whole story. The king's son was very taken with her, and seeing that such a gift was worth more than the richest dowry of any other girl, brought her to his father the king's palace and there he married her.

As for her sister, she behaved so hatefully that her own mother threw her out. The wretched girl couldn't find anyone to take her in, so she crept away and died in a corner of a wood.

MORAL

Diamonds and gold
Get us all stirred;
But there's more true worth
In a kindly word.

ANOTHER MORAL

Though it takes care to show respect
And kindness of your own accord,
More often than you might expect
Kindness brings its own reward.

CINDERELLA

THERE WAS ONCE a man who took for his second wife the most haughty, stuck-up woman you ever saw. She had two daughters of her own, just like her in everything. The husband for his part had a young daughter, but she was gentle and sweet-natured, taking after her mother, who had been the best person in the world.

The wedding was barely over when the stepmother let her temper show; she couldn't bear the young girl's goodness, for it made her own daughters seem even more hateful. She gave her the vilest household chores: it was she who cleaned the dishes and the stairs, she who scrubbed Madam's chamber, and the chambers of those little madams, her stepsisters; she slept at the top of the house in an attic, on a shabby mattress, while her sisters had luxurious boudoirs, with beds of the latest fashion, and mirrors in which they could study themselves from head to toe. The poor girl suffered it all patiently and didn't dare complain to her father, who would have scolded her, because he was completely under the woman's sway.

When she had done her work, she would retire to the

chimney corner and sit in the cinders, so that they commonly called her Cinderbutt, though the younger sister, who wasn't quite so rude as the elder, called her Cinderella. And despite everything, Cinderella in her rags was still a hundred times prettier than her sisters, for all their sumptuous clothes.

It happened that the king's son gave a ball, to which he asked all the quality; our two misses were also asked, as they cut quite a dash in the district. They were thrilled, and kept themselves very busy choosing the clothes and hairstyles which would show them off best — a new worry for Cinderella because it was she who ironed her sisters' petticoats and pleated their ruffles. They couldn't talk of anything but clothes. ''Myself,'' said the elder, ''I'll wear my red velvet gown with the English trimming.'' ''As for me,'' said the younger, ''I'll just wear a simple skirt, but to make up for that I'll have my shawl with the golden flowers, and my diamond cummerbund, which isn't the plainest ever made.''

They sent for an expert to adjust their two-layered headdresses, and bought beauty spots. They asked Cinderella for her advice, because she had such good taste; Cinderella gave them every possible help, and offered to do their hair herself, which they were pleased to accept. But while she combed, they said to her, ''Cinderella, wouldn't you like to go to the ball?''

Cinderella sighed. ''You're making fun of me, ladies, that's not my place.''

''You're right. People would have a good laugh to see a Cinderbutt at the ball.''

Anyone else but Cinderella would have tangled their hair, but she was good, and she styled it to perfection.

The sisters went nearly two days without eating, they were so excited, and they broke more than a dozen corset laces pulling them tight to get a wasp waist, and they were always at the mirror.

At last the happy day arrived, and they set off. Cinderella stared after them as long as she could, and when she could no longer see them, she began to cry. Her godmother, who saw her weeping, asked her what she wanted.

"I want . . . I want . . ." She cried so hard she couldn't finish.

Her godmother, who was a fairy, said, "You want to go to the ball, isn't that it?"

"Yes," sighed Cinderella.

"Well, if you're a good girl, I shall send you," said her godmother. She took her into her own room and told her, "Go into the garden and bring me a pumpkin."

Cinderella went right out and picked the finest she could find and took it to her godmother, without the least idea how a pumpkin could help her go to the ball. Her godmother scooped it out to a hollow skin, then tapped it with her wand, and the pumpkin was instantly turned into a beautiful gilded carriage. Then she looked in the mousetrap, where she found six live mice. She told Cinderella to lift the trap door a little, and as each mouse escaped, she struck it with her wand, and the mouse was straightaway changed into a handsome horse. They made a fine set of six dappled horses, all a lovely mouse shade.

As her godmother was having difficulty finding something she could turn into a coachman, Cinderella said, "I'll go and see if there is a rat in the rat trap, and we can make a coachman of him."

"Good idea," said her godmother, "go and see."

Cinderella brought her the rat trap, in which there were three fat rats. The fairy chose the one with the finest whiskers and with a touch transformed him into a portly coachman, with the most lavish moustache you ever saw.

"Now," she said, "go into the garden, and you'll find six lizards behind the watering can. Bring them to me."

No sooner had she fetched them in than her godmother changed them into six footmen, who climbed up behind the carriage in their brocade livery and clung there as if they had done nothing else all their lives.

The fairy said to Cinderella, "Well, now you can go to the ball. Aren't you happy?"

"Yes, but do I have to go like this, in tatters?"

Her godmother touched Cinderella with her wand, and her clothes changed into garments of gold and silver cloth, richly embroidered with jewels. Then she gave her a pair of glass slippers, the prettiest in the world.

When she was ready, she got into the carriage; but her godmother warned her on no account to stay after midnight, for if she stayed at the ball one moment longer, her carriage would turn back into a pumpkin, the horses into mice, the footmen into lizards, and her old clothes would look just as they had before.

Cinderella promised her godmother that she would leave the ball before midnight without fail, and set off, beside herself with joy.

When the prince was told that a grand princess had arrived whom nobody knew, he ran out to welcome her, and gave her his hand to step down from the carriage, and took her himself into the room where the guests were. They all fell silent; the dancing ceased; the violins stopped playing; all eyes were on the rare beauty of this unknown woman.

The only noise was a confused murmuring, "Oh! She's beautiful!"

Even the king, ancient as he was, couldn't stop looking at her and whispering to the queen that it was a long while since he'd seen anyone so lovely, so beautiful.

All the ladies studied her hair and her clothes, to have copies made the next day, if they could find such gorgeous materials and such clever dressmakers.

The prince led her to the seat next to his, and afterwards took her onto the dance floor; she danced with such grace, everyone admired her even more. There was a splendid supper, but the prince couldn't eat a thing, he was so wrapped up in her.

She went and sat near her sisters and showed them every

civility; she gave them some of the oranges and lemons the prince had given her, which surprised them very much, for they didn't recognize her at all. As they chatted, Cinderella heard the chimes mark a quarter to twelve. She immediately curtseyed to the company and left as fast as she could.

When she got home, she found her godmother, and after thanking her, told her that she wanted very much to go to the ball again on the next day, because the prince had begged her to come. Whilst she was telling her godmother everything that had happened at the ball, the two sisters knocked at the door, and Cinderella let them in.

"What a long time you've been," she told them, yawning and rubbing her eyes and stretching as if she had just woken up, though she hadn't had a sleepy thought since they left home.

"If you'd been at the ball," said one of the sisters, "you wouldn't have been wearied. There was the most beautiful princess there, the loveliest you could ever see; she was so kind to us, and gave us oranges and lemons."

Cinderella was beside herself with joy. She asked what the princess's name was, but they told her that nobody knew, that the prince was in despair and would give the whole world to know who she was. Cinderella smiled and said, "Was she really so beautiful? Gracious, you are lucky! Can't I see her? Oh dear! Miss Javotte, lend me your yellow dress, the one you wear every day."

"Lend my dress to a grimy Cinderbutt?" said Miss Javotte. "One would have to be stark mad, to be sure."

Cinderella knew very well she would refuse, and she was quite happy, because she would have been in an embarrassing fix if her sister had really agreed to lend her the dress.

The next day the two sisters
went to the ball, and Cinderella too, even more grandly
dressed than the first time.
The prince was always by
her and never stopped
talking sweet nothings;
the young lady
wasn't at all
bored, and
forgot what
her god-
mother
told
her,

with the result that she heard the first stroke of midnight when she thought it was still only eleven. She jumped up and fled, as nimbly as a doe. The prince followed her. He couldn't catch her, but she did drop one of her glass slippers, which the prince picked up tenderly.

Cinderella got home all out of breath, no carriage, no flunkeys, in her grubby clothes, with nothing left of her magnificence save a single little slipper, the mate of the one she dropped.

The palace guards were asked if they saw the princess leave. They said they saw no one leave but a badly dressed girl who looked more like a peasant than a lady.

When the two sisters returned from the ball, Cinderella asked them if they had enjoyed themselves again, and if the beautiful lady had come; they told her yes, but she had fled as midnight struck, so hastily that she had let fall one of her little glass slippers, the prettiest in the world. The prince had picked it up, and had done nothing but look at it for the rest of the ball. He was certainly head over heels in love with the lovely owner of the little slipper.

They were telling the truth. A few days later, the prince had it cried to the sound of trumpets that he would marry the girl whose foot fitted the slipper. He started by trying all the princesses, then the duchesses, and all the court, but it was no use. The slipper was brought to the two sisters, who tried everything to force their feet into the slipper, but they couldn't manage it. Cinderella, who was watching, and who recognized her own slipper, laughed and said, "Let me see if it fits me."

Her sisters burst out laughing, and jeered at her. The gentleman in charge of the slipper looked closely at Cinderella, and finding her extremely attractive, said she was right, because he'd been told to try all the girls. He made Cinderella sit down, and putting the slipper on her tiny foot, he saw it slipped on as easily, and fitted as perfectly, as if it were made of wax. The sisters were astonished, but even more so when Cinderella took the other little slipper from her pocket and put it on her foot. Then the godmother came and touched Cinderella's clothes with her wand, making them turn into garments even more stunning than all the others.

So the two sisters recognized her as the beautiful lady they had seen at the ball. They threw themselves at her feet and asked forgiveness for all the harsh treatment they had made her suffer. Cinderella raised them up, and kissed them, and forgave them with all her heart, and asked them to love her always.

She was taken to the prince dressed as she was, and he thought her even more beautiful than ever, and a few days later he married her. Cinderella, who was as good as she was beautiful, took her sisters to live in the palace, and married them the same day to two great lords of the court.

MORAL

Beauty in woman is a very rare treasure:
Of it we can never tire.
But what's worth more, a priceless pleasure,
Is charm, which we must all admire.

That wise instructress, the godmother,
While dressing her fit for a queen
Was giving her power to charm another;
That is what this story means.

Ladies, better than teased-up hair is
To win a heart, and conquer a ball.
Charm is the true gift of the fairies;
Without it you've nothing; with it, all.

ANOTHER MORAL

It is no doubt a great advantage
To have shrewdness, wit, and courage;
To be well born, with every sense
And have all sorts of other talents
Which Heaven gives you for your share.
But with or without them, when all is said,
They'll never help you get ahead
Unless to spread your talents farther
You've a willing godmother, or godfather.

TUFTY RICKY

THERE WAS ONCE a queen who had a son so ugly and malformed that for a long time people wondered whether he was human. A fairy who was present at the birth promised that, because he would be very clever, everyone would like him nonetheless. She also added that, thanks to the gift she had just given him, he would be able to share his intelligence with the person he loved the most.

So the poor queen felt a bit better about having brought such an ugly brat into the world. And it was true, the child was soon prattling so merrily and wittily, and all his actions had something so charming about them, that everyone was won over. I forgot to say that he came into the world with a little tuft of hair on his head, so that he was known as Tufty Ricky, since Ricky was the family name.

After seven or eight years, the queen of a nearby kingdom gave birth to two daughters. The first who was born was more beautiful than the day; the queen was so overjoyed that people feared for her wits. The same fairy who was present at the birth of little Tufty Ricky was there, and in order to calm the queen, she told her that this little princess would not be very bright; she would be as stupid as she was beautiful. The queen was deeply mortified by this. But a few moments later she suffered an even greater sorrow, for the second daughter she gave birth to turned out to be extremely ugly.

"Don't be so upset, my lady," the fairy said to her. "Your daughter will have other compensations. She will be so clever that people will scarcely notice her lack of beauty."

"As God wills," replied the queen. "But is there really no way of giving a spark of intelligence to the elder who is so beautiful?"

"I can't do anything for her as regards her brains," said the fairy, "but as far as beauty is concerned, I can do a great deal. Since there is nothing I would not do to please you, I am going to give her this gift, that she will be able to make the person she loves as handsome as she is beautiful."

As the two princesses grew up, their perfections grew with them, and everyone everywhere spoke only of the beauty of the elder and the wit of the younger. It is true also that their defects, too, increased greatly with age. The younger grew uglier virtually as you looked at her, and the elder became stupider from one day to the next. She either did not reply to questions she was asked or gave some idiotic answer.

She was also so clumsy that she could not arrange a few pieces of china on a mantelpiece without breaking one, nor drink a glass of water without spilling half on her clothes. Even though beauty is a great advantage in a young person, nevertheless the younger sister almost always outshone the elder in company. At first people would throng round the elder to gaze at her and admire her, but soon after they would turn to the clever one to be entertained by her witty thoughts. It was astonishing how after less than a quarter of an hour the elder would be abandoned and everyone would have gathered around the younger. Even though the elder sister was very stupid indeed, she noticed this and would have given up all her beauty with no regrets in return for half of her sister's intelligence. The queen, however good she was, could not help reproaching her many times for her stupidity, and the poor princess thought she would die of grief and shame.

One day the elder princess had hidden herself away in a wood to weep over her misfortune when she saw a little man coming who was very ugly and peculiar-looking, but dressed in the latest fashion. It was the young prince, Tufty Ricky. He had fallen in love with her from the portraits of her that were available all over the world, and he had left his father's kingdom in the hope of being able to see her and talk to her.

He was delighted to meet her alone, and he approached her with all the respect and politeness imaginable. After paying her the usual compliments, he noticed how sad she was, and said to her, "I cannot understand, miss, how anyone as lovely as you are could be as sad as you seem to be; for though I can boast of having seen an infinite number of attractive people, I can say that I have never seen anyone whose beauty even approaches yours."

"That is very kind of you, sir," replied the princess and left it at that.

"Beauty," continued Tufty Ricky, "is such an asset that everything else is insignificant beside it. When you have beauty, nothing can trouble you much."

The princess said, "I would rather be as ugly as you and be intelligent than have the beauty I have and be as stupid as I am."

"But there is no better proof of intelligence than for a person to believe that she does not possess it, for it is the very nature of wit that the more one has, the less one thinks one has."

"I don't know about that," said the princess, "but I do know that I am so stupid I want to die."

"If that is all that is upsetting you, then I can easily put an end to your suffering."

"How can you?" said the princess.

"Well," said Tufty Ricky, "I have the power to give as much intelligence as anyone could possibly know what to do with to the person I love the most. And as you are that person, it is up to you. If you agree to marry me, you can be as intelligent as anyone would ever want to be." The princess was taken aback and did not reply. Tufty Ricky said, "I can see that this proposal troubles you, and I am not surprised, but I will give you a whole year to think about it."

The princess had so little intelligence, and at the same time such a great desire to have some, that she thought the end of the year would never come, so she accepted his proposal right away. She had no sooner promised Tufty Ricky that she would marry him in a year to the day, than she felt utterly changed.

She found she could say anything she wanted, in a sophisticated and natural way. From that moment, she began flirting with Tufty Ricky, chatting away so brightly that Tufty Ricky wondered if he hadn't given her more intelligence than he had kept for himself.

When she returned to the palace, the whole court was baffled by such a sudden and extraordinary change. For every silly thing they had heard her say before, she now said something well thought out and witty. The whole court was overjoyed about it. But the younger sister's nose was put out of joint, because now that she no longer had the advantage of intelligence over her sister, compared to her she now seemed nothing but a fright.

The king let himself be guided by his elder daughter's advice and sometimes even held council in her rooms. The news of this change spread everywhere, and all the young princes of the nearby kingdoms made every effort to win her love and almost all asked for her hand in marriage; but not one of them did she find intelligent enough, and she listened to them all without committing herself to any one of them. However, one came along who was so powerful, so rich, so witty, and so handsome that she could not help feeling well disposed toward him. Her father noticed this and said that he gave her the right to make her own choice of husband; she merely had to choose.

The brighter one is, the more difficult it is to come to a decision on this particular matter; so, having thanked her father, she asked him to give her some time to think it over. By chance, she went walking in the same wood where she had met Tufty Ricky, hoping to think privately about what she had to do. While she was walking, deep in thought, she heard a dull sound

from beneath her feet, as if people were
bustling about down there. When she listened
more carefully, she heard one person saying,
"Bring me that pot," and another, "Give me that
pan," and another, "Put wood on the fire."

The earth opened up as she listened, and beneath her feet she
saw what looked like a huge kitchen, full of cooks and kitchen
boys and all the staff necessary to prepare a magnificent feast. A
band of twenty or thirty spit-turners trooped out and set up a
very long table in one of the avenues in the wood. With their
chef's caps perched on the sides of their heads and their basting
implements in their hands, they all set to work with a will, in
time to a merry song. The princess, astonished by this spectacle,
asked them who they were working for.

"Madam," replied the head cook, "it's for Prince Tufty
Ricky, for his wedding feast tomorrow." The princess
was more surprised than ever. In a flash she
remembered that it was a year to the day
since she had promised to marry Tufty
Ricky, and she felt as if she were

going to faint. The reason why she had not remembered was that when she made that promise she had been a stupid creature, and when she took on the new intelligence the prince had given her, she had forgotten all her old silliness. She had taken only about thirty more steps on her walk when Tufty Ricky appeared before her, gallant and magnificent, like a prince about to be married.

"Here I am, madam," he said, "keeping my word to the letter, and I have no doubt that you have come to keep yours too and, by giving me your hand in marriage, to make me the happiest of men."

"I will be quite frank with you," said the princess, "and confess to you that I have not yet made up my mind on that score, and that I do not think I will ever be able to take the decision you long for."

"You astonish me, madam," said Tufty Ricky.

"I can well believe it," said the princess, "and of course, if I were dealing with a brute or an unintelligent man, I would feel extremely awkward. A princess has only her word, such a man would say, and since you promised, you must marry me. But since the man I am speaking to is the most intelligent man in the world, I am sure that he will listen to reason. You know that when I was stupider than a beast, even then I had difficulty deciding whether to marry you. How can you expect that with the intelligence you have given me, which makes me even more particular about the people I mix with than I was before, I should take a decision today which I could not take then? If you intended to marry me anyhow, you were very wrong to take away my stupidity and make me see more clearly than I used to."

"If a stupid man," replied Tufty Ricky, "would be considered justified in reproaching you for breaking your word, as you have just said, why do you expect me not to make use of the same argument, since my entire happiness is at stake? Is it reasonable that intelligent people should live in a worse state than people who have no wit at all? Can you claim this, you who have so much intelligence and desired it so much? But please, let's come to the point: apart from my ugliness, is there anything about me that you do not like? Are you unhappy about my birth, my intelligence, my character, or my manners?"

"In no way," replied the princess. "I love all those aspects of you that you have just mentioned."

"If that is the case," answered Tufty Ricky, "then I am to be happy after all, since you can make me the most attractive of all men."

"How can that be?" said the princess.

"It can be," replied Tufty Ricky, "if you love me enough to wish it to be. And besides, the same fairy that on the day of my birth gave me the gift of making the person whom I loved intelligent, also gave you the gift of making the person you love attractive."

"If that is so," said the princess, "I wish with all my heart that you should become the handsomest, most attractive prince in the world. I give you the gift if it is in my power." The princess had no sooner uttered these words than Tufty Ricky appeared before her as the handsomest, comeliest, and most attractive man ever seen.

There are those who claim that there was no fairy spell at work here but that love alone caused this transformation. They say that the princess thought about her lover's faithfulness, his charm, and all the good qualities of his soul and mind and no longer saw the deformity of his body, nor the ugliness of his face. With his humpback he now looked to her like nothing other than a man simply arching his back; and whereas before she had thought he limped horribly, now there was merely a lilt in his step which she found utterly charming. They also say that his eyes, which squinted, now only seemed all the more sparkling, and the squint itself seemed a sign of raging passion. Even his large red nose seemed to her to have something soldierly and heroic about it.

Whatever the truth of the matter, the princess promised there and then to marry him, provided that he had the consent of her father the king. When the king knew of his daughter's feeling for Tufty Ricky, whom in any case he knew to be a wise and thoughtful prince, he accepted him as his son-in-law with great pleasure.

The following day the wedding took place, just as Tufty Ricky had planned and according to the orders he had given long before.

MORAL

This tale is not so very fanciful,
For what's true once is true forever;
Those we love are always beautiful,
Those we love are always clever.

ANOTHER MORAL

Though nature paints some people's features
In lovely tints beyond the reach of art,
Still there's something hidden in all creatures
For love to find, and melt the heart.

HOP O' MY THUMB

THERE WAS ONCE a woodcutter and his wife who had seven children, all sons. The oldest was ten years old and the youngest only seven. People were astonished that the woodcutter had managed to have so many children in so little time, but the reason was that his wife became pregnant quickly and never had fewer than two sons at once.

The woodcutter and his wife were very poor, and their seven children caused them a lot of hardship because none of them was old enough yet to earn a living. What troubled the couple further was that the youngest was extremely delicate and never uttered a word. They took this for a sign of stupidity, whereas in fact it was because he was so gentle. He was very small indeed. When he came into the world he was scarcely larger than your thumb, and so he was called Hop o' My Thumb. This poor child was the scapegoat for the whole household and was always in the wrong. Nevertheless, he was the most intelligent and knowledgeable of all the brothers, and if he didn't speak much he was a good listener.

There came a year of such terrible famine that these poor

people could no longer feed their children. One evening, when the children were in bed and the woodcutter was by the fire with his wife, he said to her, his heart pinched with sorrow, "We cannot feed our children anymore. I couldn't bear to see them die of hunger before my eyes, so I've decided to take them to the woods tomorrow and lose them. It should be very easy. While they are enjoying themselves gathering wood, all we have to do is run away without them seeing us."

"Ah!" cried his wife. "Could you abandon your own children?" Her husband tried to convince her of their extreme poverty but she would not consent to losing the children: she was poor, but she was their mother. However, when she realized what agony it would be to watch them die of hunger, she gave in and went to bed in tears.

Hop o' My Thumb heard all that they said, for their voices woke him, and hearing that they were talking about household affairs, he had got up quietly and slipped beneath his father's stool in order to listen without being seen. He went back to bed and didn't sleep for the rest of the night, thinking what to do. He got up early and went to a stream where he filled his pockets with tiny white pebbles and then came back to the house.

Everyone set off. Hop o' My Thumb did not tell his brothers anything of what he knew. They went into a part of the forest so thick that you couldn't see someone else only ten paces away. The woodcutter started to cut logs, and his children scattered to collect sticks for kindling. When the father and mother could see that the boys were busy at their task, they crept away unnoticed and then fled down a little path.

When the children saw they were alone, they started to cry and bawl. Hop o' My Thumb let them shout. He knew full well how they were going to find their way home, for, as they walked along, he had dropped the little white pebbles he had in his pockets and marked the path. So he said to them, "Don't be afraid, brothers. Our mother and father have left us here, but I will take you back home. Just follow me."

They followed him, and he took them right back to their house by the same path they had taken into the forest. At first they didn't dare go in, but they all huddled round the door to eavesdrop on what their mother and father were saying.

At the moment that the woodcutter and his wife had arrived home, the local squire had sent them ten sovereigns which he had owed them for so long that they had given up hope of ever being paid. This was life itself to poor people dying of hunger. The woodcutter sent his wife off to buy meat. As they had not eaten for so long, the two of them could only manage a third of what she had bought. When they were full, the woodcutter's wife said, "Alas, where are my poor children now? They could have eaten their fill from our leavings. It was your idea to get rid of them, William. I said we would regret it. What is happening now in that forest? Oh God! Perhaps the wolves have eaten them already. How could you be so cruel as to abandon your children like that?"

Eventually the woodcutter lost his temper, for she repeated more than twenty times that they would regret it and that she had told him so. He threatened to beat her if she did not shut up. The woodcutter was just as upset as his wife, but she was annoying him. He was like many men who are very fond of women who talk sense but very irritated by the ones who are always right. The woodcutter's wife said through her tears, "Alas! Where are my children now? My poor children!"

She said it so loud that the children at the door heard it and started to shout all together, "Here we are! Here we are!"

She ran to open the door. She kissed them and said, "Oh, how happy I am to see you again, my dear children. You must be tired and hungry; and Peter, my pet, you're all dirty! Here, let me clean you up a little." Peter was her oldest son, and she loved him more than the others as he had reddish hair like hers.

The children all sat at table and ate with an appetite that delighted their mother and father. They told of their fear in the forest, all speaking more or less at the same time.

These poor folk were thrilled to have their children with them again, and this joy lasted as long as the ten sovereigns lasted. But when the money had been spent, they started to worry again. They decided once more to abandon the children and, to make sure this time, they led them much farther into the forest than they had the first time.

But they couldn't plot so secretly that Hop o' My Thumb couldn't hear them, and he planned to put matters right as before. However, even though he got up early to gather the little pebbles, he was thwarted as he found the door of the house double-locked. He couldn't think what to do until the woodcutter's wife gave each child a hunk of bread for his breakfast. Hop o' My Thumb decided he could use his bread instead of pebbles by dropping crumbs of it all along the paths they took, and so he stuffed his piece into his pocket.

The father and mother took the boys into the thickest and darkest part of the forest and, as soon as they got there, took a

hidden shortcut
and left them. Hop o' My Thumb
did not worry too much, as he thought he
could easily find the way back using the trail of
bread he had left. But to his surprise he could not trace a single
crumb, as birds had come and eaten them all up.

So there they were with things going from bad to worse, for the more they walked, the more lost they became and the farther they went into the forest. Night fell and a huge wind came up, which frightened them horribly. They thought they could hear on all sides the howling of wolves coming to eat them. They scarcely dared to speak or turn their heads. Then a heavy rain started to fall, soaking them to the skin. They skidded at each step and slipped into the mud and then got up again all filthy, not knowing where to put their hands.

Hop o' My Thumb climbed a tree to see if he could find anything out. He looked in all directions and then saw a tiny glimmer like a candle flame, but a long way off, beyond the forest. He came down from the tree, and when he was on the ground again he could see nothing anymore, which dismayed him. However, when he and his brothers had walked for a while toward the light he had seen, he saw the light again, just as they came out of the trees. They finally reached a house where a candle was burning, but not without plenty of scares along the way, for they lost sight of it every time they went into a dip in the ground.

They knocked at the door and a good woman came and answered. She asked them what they wanted, and Hop o' My Thumb said they were poor children who had got lost in the forest and begged a bed for the night. When the woman saw how sweet they all were, she began to cry and said to them, "My poor children! To have come to such a place! Don't you know that this is the home of an ogre who eats children?"

"Oh dear!" cried Hop o' My Thumb, who was trembling with fear, just like his brothers. "What are we to do? The wolves in the forest will surely gobble us up tonight if you do not take us in. And as that is the case, we would prefer this gentleman to eat us. Perhaps he will take pity on us, if you are kind enough to beg him to." The ogre's wife, who thought she could hide them from her husband until the following morning, let them in and took them to warm themselves up in front of a good fire, where there was an entire sheep turning on a spit for the ogre's supper.

They were just beginning to get warm when they heard three or four great knocks on the door. It was the ogre coming back. Immediately the wife hid them under the bed and went to open the door. First of all, the ogre asked if supper was ready and if wine had been poured, and then sat at the table. The sheep was still all bloody, but the meat only seemed the better for it to the ogre. He sniffed to the right and sniffed to the left, saying he could smell fresh flesh. His wife said, "It must be the calf I have just prepared for cooking that you can smell."

"I smell fresh flesh, I tell you," said the ogre, looking at his wife suspiciously, "and there is something here I don't understand." With that he got up from the table and went straight over to the bed.

"Aha!" he said. "So that's how you were hoping to trick me, cursed woman. I don't know why I don't eat you too. Consider yourself lucky you're such a tough old cow. But this game here is choice and tender enough for me to serve up to three ogre friends of mine who are coming to visit shortly." He pulled the children out from under the bed, one after the other. The poor children fell on their knees, begging for mercy, but they were dealing with a cruel ogre who, far from feeling pity for them, was already devouring them with his eyes, telling his wife that they would make delectable snacks when she had prepared a good sauce for them.

He went and fetched a large knife, and as he approached those poor children, he sharpened it on a long stone which he held in his left hand. He had already grabbed one of the children when his wife said to him, "Just look at the time! Wouldn't it be better to slaughter them tomorrow morning?"

"Shut up!" said the ogre. "They'll only be more bruised."

"But you've got so much meat left," his wife went on. "Look, there's plenty for dinner: a calf, two sheep, and half a pig."

"You're right," said the ogre. "Give them a good supper so

89

that they don't lose weight, and then put them straight to bed."

The good woman was overjoyed and gave them an excellent supper, but they were so terrified they couldn't eat. As for the ogre, he began drinking, delighted to have such good food to offer his friends. He drank twelve glasses more than usual, until his head began to spin and he had to go and lie down.

The ogre had seven daughters who were still little girls. These little ogresses had lovely rosy complexions, because they ate fresh flesh like their father, but they had mean little round eyes, sharp noses, and huge mouths full of long, pointy teeth with gaps between them. They were not yet entirely evil, but they showed promise, and were already fond of biting little babies and sucking their blood. They had been put to bed early, and all seven were in a large bed, each with a golden crown on her head. In the same room was another bed of the same size. It was in this bed that the ogre's wife put the seven little boys before she went to join her husband in bed.

Hop o' My Thumb had noticed that the ogre's daughters had gold crowns on their heads. Fearing that the ogre might regret not having cut the boys' throats that very evening, he got up toward midnight, took the nightcaps off his brothers' heads and off his own, and slipped them onto the heads of the ogre's seven daughters, having first taken off their golden crowns. These he placed on his brothers' heads and on his own, so that the ogre would take them for his daughters and his daughters for the boys whose throats he wanted to cut.

The trick worked just as he had hoped, for the ogre woke up around midnight and regretted having put off till the morrow what he could have done the same day. So he flung himself from the bed and grabbed his large knife.

"Let's just see how our dear little things are getting on," he said. "I'll not make the same mistake twice." He crept up to his daughters' room and went over to the bed where the little boys were lying all asleep, apart from Hop o' My Thumb, who was terrified when he felt the ogre's hand groping for his head just as he had touched the heads of all the brothers.

The ogre felt the golden crowns. "Really! That was a near miss! I see I must have drunk far too much last night." He then felt his way to the bed of his little daughters, and there his fingers touched the nightcaps belonging to the boys.

"Ah, you scamps! Is that where you've got to? Let's be having you!" As he said these words, he calmly slit his seven daughters' throats, and then went smugly back to bed with his wife.

As soon as Hop o' My Thumb heard the ogre snoring, he woke his brothers and told them to dress quickly and follow him. They crept quietly into the garden and over the wall. They kept running almost all night, trembling all the while and not knowing where they were heading.

When the ogre woke he said to his wife, "Go up and dress those little fellows from yesterday for this evening." The ogress was astonished by her husband's kindness, not realizing at all from his tone that he meant her to dress them for the table, but thinking he wanted her to dress them in clothes. She went upstairs where she was horrified to find her seven daughters swimming in their own blood, with their throats cut. As any mother would when faced with such a sight, she fainted clean away. The ogre fretted that his wife was taking so long over the task he had set her, and came upstairs to help her. He was no less astounded than his wife when he set eyes on that frightful scene.

"Oh! What have I done?" he exclaimed. "But I'll make those wretches pay, and straightaway too." He threw a pot of water in his wife's face to bring her round, then said, "Bring me my seven-league boots. Quickly! So I can catch them."

He set off across the country-side and, having covered a huge distance in all directions, finally came upon the path where the poor children were walking along, barely a hundred paces from their father's house. They could see the ogre striding from mountain to mountain and crossing rivers as easily as the smallest stream. Hop o' My Thumb spotted a hollow boulder nearby, hid his six brothers inside, and crammed himself in there too, all the while keeping an eye on the ogre.

The ogre was exhausted

after all that futile walking, for seven-league boots are very tiring to wear, and wanted to take a rest. By chance he sat down on the very boulder where the little boys were hiding.

As he was too worn out to go on, he soon fell asleep and started snoring so ferociously that the poor children were just as afraid as if he was holding his large knife about to cut their throats. Hop o' My Thumb was the bravest. He told his brothers to flee to their parents' house while the ogre was fast asleep and not to worry about him at all. They didn't need telling twice, and soon they were safe at the house.

Hop o' My Thumb crept up to the ogre, eased off the seven-league boots, and put them on himself. They seemed far too big, but as they were magic, they had the power to get bigger and smaller according to the size of the person wearing them, so they fitted his feet and legs like gloves.

He went straight to the ogre's house where he found the ogre's wife weeping beside her dead daughters. Hop o' My Thumb said to her, ''Your husband is in grave danger: he has been captured by a band of robbers who have sworn to kill him if he doesn't give them all his gold and silver. Just as they were pressing the knife to his throat, he spotted me and begged me to come and warn you about what is happening to him and to tell you to give me everything of value that he has, without holding anything back, because otherwise they will kill him without pity. As the matter was so urgent, he wanted me to wear his seven-league boots. I wore them for speed but also to show you that I'm no impostor.''

The good woman was terribly flustered, and hurried to give him everything she had; for the ogre was her husband, even though he did eat little children. So Hop o' My Thumb, laden with all the ogre's riches, returned to his father's house, where he was welcomed with great joy.

There are many people who do not agree with this ending to the story. They say Hop o' My Thumb did not steal from the ogre, but that he didn't worry about taking the seven-league boots since the ogre only used them for chasing little children. These people assure me that they know this from a good source and even that they learned it eating and drinking in the woodcutter's house. They insist that when Hop o' My Thumb had put on the ogre's boots, he went off to the court, where he knew that everyone was very anxious about an army which was ten leagues away and about the outcome of a battle they were engaged in. They say he went to the king and said that if it would help, he could bring back news of the army before the end of the day. The king promised him a large sum of money if he achieved this. Hop o' My Thumb brought back the news before that same evening, and once it was known that he had carried out his first errand, he began to make good money. The king paid him very well for taking orders to the army. Also an endless number of women gave him all he wanted in return for news from their lovers, and that was where he earned most. He found a few women who gave him letters for their husbands, but they paid so badly and there was so little of such work that he didn't even bother to account for what he earned in that area. Having been a courier for some while and having amassed a great deal of wealth, he went back to his father, and it is impossible to imagine the joy with which he was welcomed. He made his entire family wealthy and accepted new titles for his father and brothers, and in this way established them all and at the same time continued to serve at court.

MORAL

Boys who are bright and look all right
Are always welcome to most folk,
While one who's weak or doesn't speak
Will be the butt of every joke.
But for all that the little brat
May turn out useful, when you're broke.

PATIENT GRISELDA

LADIES NOWADAYS HAVE everything according to their wishes. They do recognize that patience is a virtue, but they prefer their husbands to observe it rather than themselves. But that's no reason to make a laughingstock of poor, old-fashioned Griselda, whose story I am about to tell you.

At the foot of the famous mountains where the Po escapes from its reedy bed and sends waters springing across the fields of the surrounding countryside, there lived a young and valiant prince, the pride of the country. Heaven had blessed him with every one of those great gifts which usually occur singly, and are given only to great kings.

Intelligent and strong, he was both brave and sensitive, loving the arts as well as war and victory. And above those great actions that make a man's name live in history, he valued the small kindnesses that simply make someone happy.

Only one thing clouded his life and made him sad. He simply could not trust any woman. He thought all women were faithless and deceitful, and that, however virtuous they appeared, they were all dizzy with pride and only wanted to lord it over men. He swore he would never marry.

So he spent his mornings putting the world to rights, and his afternoons hunting. He said that the boars and bears were nothing like as frightening as women, whom he avoided at all costs.

His subjects constantly pressed him to marry, so that he could found a dynasty which would continue his gentle and thoughtful rule. But he always refused. "Women only want one thing," he said, "and that is to lay down the law. I will marry only if you find me a young beauty without pride or vanity, who is totally obedient, who will put up with anything, and who has no will of her own. If you find such a woman, I will have her."

With that, the prince jumped on his horse and set off for the hunt. In the excitement of the chase, the prince was separated from his fellow huntsmen, and rode so far down a side path that he could no longer hear the sound of the hounds and the horns. The path led to a lovely, secret place of clear springs and dark greenery, which filled his heart with joy. And when he looked about him, he saw the loveliest girl he had ever seen.

She was a young shepherdess, spinning by the side of a stream. She could have tamed the most savage heart. Her skin was like lilies, and her natural bloom had been protected by the woodland shade. Her mouth was as pretty as a child's, and her eyes, with their soft dark lashes, were bluer than the sky and filled with light.

The prince, transported, slipped into the trees to gaze on her beauty, but the noise he made caused her to turn toward him. As soon as she saw him, she blushed violently. Beneath the rosy veil of this adorable shame, the prince glimpsed the simplicity,

the sweet-
ness, and the
sincerity of which
he had thought women
incapable.

He was suddenly shy, as he had
never been before. He approached
her timidly and asked her in a trembling voice
whether the hunt had passed that way.

"Nothing has passed this way, lord," she said. "But do not
worry. I will guide you back to a familiar path."

"I cannot believe my luck," he said. "I have been coming to
these woods for so long, and yet until today I knew nothing of
their most precious treasure." As he spoke, he bent down to the
damp bank of the stream to drink the flowing water.

"My lord, wait a moment," she said, and running swiftly to
her hut, she fetched him a cup. No precious goblet ever seemed
as beautiful to him as that simple clay cup. And when the
shepherdess led him back to a path he knew, the prince
took care to remember every twist and turn of the
route, so that he could always find his way back to
her.

After that he always took care to lose the hunt

99

and visit the shepherdess, whose name was Griselda. She lived quietly with her father in a simple hut, drinking the milk from their flocks and making their fleeces into clothes.

The more he saw her, the more he fell in love with the bright beauties of her soul. And so he announced to his council that he would, after all, marry. "I will not take a wife from a foreign land," he said, "but from among my subjects. She will be beautiful, wise, and well born, but I will not say who she is until the wedding day."

The preparations went forward for the great day, which was to be the grandest wedding ever held. Everyone was full of joy, and everyone lined the streets to watch the prince come from his palace to the church. They were all astonished to see him, instead, take the first turning into the forest, as he did every day. "Just look," they said, "hunting is still his first love!"

Soon he reached Griselda's hut. She had put on her best dress, and was going, like everyone else, to see the wedding.

"Where are you off to in such a hurry?" said the prince. "There's no need to rush. The wedding can't happen without you." And then he told her that he loved her, and asked her to marry him. At first she thought he was making fun of her, but he told her he was completely serious. "But you must promise to obey me in all things." And she promised that his will would be her law.

The shepherdess was soon dressed in wedding finery and seated in a great carriage made of ivory and gold, beside the prince her lover. The crowds cheered them, and in the church they were married before all the people.

Everyone took Griselda for a princess, for her wit was such that she soon learned all the manners of the court. With her lively intelligence and common sense, she was soon leading all the ladies of the court as easily as she had led her flock in the wood.

Before a year was out, their marriage had been blessed by a baby girl, who was the delight of both her father and her mother.

But gradually, amid all this happiness, the prince's old doubts began to nag at him. He wondered if all her goodness was not just a trap to make a fool of him, and his tormented spirit began to nurture jealous suspicions, as lovingly as Griselda nursed the little princess.

He began to follow her around and try to needle, upset, and alarm her, to prove to himself that she wasn't really as perfect as she seemed. After all, he told himself, if her virtue is real, bad treatment will only strengthen it. So he kept her locked up in a dark room, and never let her join in any of the fun of the court. He demanded back all the pretty gifts he had given her in their happy days, and tried to make her miserable.

But Griselda did not complain. I'm sure this is all for my own good, she thought; true happiness comes through suffering.

It was no comfort to the prince to see her obey unstintingly all his decrees. He still thought her virtue was false. He saw how much she loved the little princess, and decided that this was where he could make a real test. So he told Griselda that he must take the princess away from her, to prevent her learning bad habits from her mother. And he sent a servant to take the child away.

To tear away the child or the heart from the bosom of such a loving mother would cause the same pain; but nevertheless Griselda submitted. Ah! What bitter sorrow was hers!

The child was taken to a convent, to be brought up by nuns who did not know who she was.

The prince felt ashamed at what he had done, and went out hunting, fearing to see Griselda again, as one might fear meeting a fierce tigress whose cub has been taken from her. But on his return she treated him with the same sweetness, affection, and love as always.

So two days later, to hurt her even more, the prince told her the child was dead.

The news struck her to the heart with grief. But when she saw her husband grow pale, she seemed to forget her sorrow and think only of how to console his false grief. Her goodness, warmth, and love nearly melted the prince, and he wanted to tell her that the child was still alive; but his anger rose, and he told her fiercely that she mustn't tell anyone what had happened; it would be no use.

For the next fifteen years they lived happily together. To be sure he sometimes amused himself by trying to upset her, but it was only a whim to stop her love dying, like the blacksmith who sprinkles a little water on the brazier as he works, to redouble the heat.

Meanwhile the young princess was growing up as witty, wise, sweet, and innocent as her mother, and as proud and clever as her father, and turning as well into a perfect beauty. She caught the eye of a young nobleman of the court, a handsome, brave young man whom the prince had long had his eye on as a worthy son-in-law. But when the two young people fell in love, he was gripped by a strange desire to have them pay for their great happiness with cruel torments.

I would like to make them happy, he said to himself, but

savage distress will make their passion constant. That is how I tested my wife, and proved her goodness and wisdom.

So he made a public declaration that as he had no descendants, since his daughter had died shortly after birth, he must look elsewhere for happiness. He would marry again, and his bride would be a girl of noble birth who had been raised in innocence in a convent.

It is easy to imagine how cruel this frightful announcement seemed to the two young lovers. Then, showing neither regret nor sorrow, the prince told his faithful wife that he must separate from her, as the people, outraged at her low birth, required him to make a more worthy marriage. "You must go back to your thatched hut," he said, "and be a shepherdess again."

Griselda heard the sentence pronounced without complaint, though inside she was full of suffering. "You are my husband, lord, and master," she said "and however terrible your will, I must obey." She retired to her room, stripped herself of her rich garments, and put on again the simple garb of a shepherdess. She took her leave of the prince, saying, "I beg your pardon for having displeased you in some way. Forgive me, and I will live happily in my hut, and pray to God a hundred times a day to cover you with glory and riches and grant your every desire." Love nourished on caresses is not more passionate than hers was.

Such faithful love nearly moved the prince to abandon his plan, but he hardened his heart, and told her, "I have forgotten the past, and am happy that you have repented. Come, it is time to leave."

Griselda and her father went back to their hut in the wood,

and lived as they had before. Spinning by the same waters where the prince had found her, Griselda's heart was at peace, and without bitterness.

Then her husband sent word for her to come to see him. "Griselda," he said, "in order to make the young princess I am going to marry tomorrow happy, I want you to prepare our apartment. You know how I like things; use all your skill to please me and the young princess, whom I love tenderly."

Then the young princess arrived, more lovely than ever. When Griselda saw her she felt a sweet transport of motherly love deep in her heart. The memory of time past and happy days was awakened in her heart. "Alas!" she said to herself. "If God had listened to my prayers, my daughter would have been almost that age and perhaps as beautiful."

At that moment she felt such a strong, powerful love for the young princess that, as soon as she had gone, she went to the prince and told him, "My lord, bear with me when I tell you that this charming princess that you are to marry, who has been raised in ease, glory, and pomp, will not be able to endure the same treatment I have received from you. She would die from it. Poverty hardened me to suffering, and I could bear any misfortune without a murmur. But this girl who has never known pain will die at the first harsh word. My lord, I beg you to treat her gently."

The prince replied severely, "Concern yourself with serving me according to your abilities. A simple shepherdess should not preach to a prince." At these words Griselda lowered her eyes and left without a word.

Then the nobles invited for the wedding began to arrive, and the prince led them all into a magnificent hall. Then he addressed them: "Who could imagine that this young lady, whom marriage is going to turn into a princess, would not be happy? But she is not. And who could think that this young warrior would not be happy to see her wed his prince? But he is not. Who would think that Griselda, justly angry, would not weep and despair? But she has not complained at all. She consents to everything, and nothing has been able to push her patience to the limit. Who, finally, would imagine that anything could please me more than to marry this charming girl? Yet if I were to do so, I would be the unhappiest prince alive.

"For this lovely girl is my daughter, and I give her in marriage to this young noble, who loves her as she loves him. And

Griselda, my wise, faithful wife, whom I have driven away so unworthily, I now take back, so that I can put right, with everything that is sweetest that love can offer, the harsh, barbaric treatment that she has received from my jealous spirit. I shall work even harder to make her happy than I did to make her miserable."

Suddenly the sky seemed to clear of black cloud, and let the sunshine through. The prince led the young princess to her mother, who was so overcome with joy that she could barely feel anything at all. Her heart had been strong enough to bear any pain, but could not bear this joy. All she could do was stand there and weep.

"You will have plenty of time to satisfy your tenderness as a mother," the prince said to her. "For now, put back on the clothes that your station demands. We have a wedding to go to."

And the young couple were married with much rejoicing. Through all the feasts, games, and dances, everyone looked at Griselda, whose patience had been proved so well. Everyone was so delighted they even praised the prince, who by his cruelty had shown everyone how good she was.

MORAL

Suffering brings out the best
And the worst in everyone.
When hard times put us to the test,
We learn if we are weak or strong.

DONKEYSKIN

THERE WAS ONCE a great and wise king, ruler of a rich
and peaceful country. What's more, his faithful queen
was so loving and beautiful that he was even happier
being her husband than he was being king. And their only
daughter was the perfect child of a perfect marriage.

Even the stables of his palace were magnificent. Visitors were
always amazed to find, among the handsome horses, a donkey,
waving his long ears in the most luxurious stall. And no
wonder, for this precious donkey never let fall any dung, and
each morning his litter was strewn instead with many gold
coins.

Now God sometimes tires of making people happy, and
always mixes some misfortune with good luck, like rain with
sun. The queen fell ill, and neither the learned doctors nor the
quacks could do anything for her.

When the queen felt her end was near, she beckoned her
husband to her. "Promise me," she said, "when I die, if you
wish to marry again—"

"No, no, my love, never!" said the king.

"But if you do," she continued, "give me your word at least that you will never marry someone unless she is more beautiful, and wiser, than I." For the queen was so vain she thought this promise meant the king would never marry again.

The weeping king gave his word, and the queen died in his arms. His sobs wracked the whole palace, and it seemed such a sorrow could never be consoled. But great storms do not last long, and within a few months the king was over his grief, and casting his eye around for a likely wife.

But there was no woman the equal of the dead queen, not in the court nor in the country, not in the town nor in the lands nearby. The king returned home from his search at his wits' end. And there, in his own apartments, he finally saw the woman of his dreams: a young girl with an edge of fresh beauty which outshone even the queen, whom she very much resembled. And so the king fell madly in love with his own daughter.

The poor girl didn't know what to do. So she set off to consult her fairy godmother and tell her the sorrow of her heart. The fairy godmother said, "Do not worry. Do as I say and no harm can come to you. Although your father has this mad desire, you can refuse him without disobeying him. Tell him that before your heart can abandon itself to his love, he must give you a dress like the sky. For all his wealth and power, even if heaven is on his side he could never do that."

The young princess went straight to her lovelorn father and, trembling, told him this. He summoned the best dressmakers in the land and told them that if they did not bring him a dress like the sky, they would all be hanged.

Next morning, the dress was brought. The princess was riven

with joy and pain, for the dress was the blue of a summer sky filled with golden clouds.

Her fairy godmother whispered to her, "Princess, ask him for a dress that glimmers like the moon; he won't be able to give you that."

The princess made her request, and the king instructed the dressmakers. Next morning, they brought him the dress, and it glowed with all the moon's pale beauty. The princess was overwhelmed, but her fairy godmother told her to ask for one more gift. So she told the king, "I will never be happy in my heart until I have a dress that outshines the sun."

Once again, the dress was brought, and it dazzled every eye, as if the very sun had come into the room. The princess was struck dumb, but her fairy godmother whispered in her ear, "Don't stop now; you've made a good start. It's no wonder your father can give you these gorgeous dresses, for he has that donkey in his stable, constantly filling his purse with gold. Ask him for the donkey's skin. You'll not be given *that*, unless I'm very much mistaken."

But wise as the fairy was, she didn't understand how rash and careless human passion is, and no sooner was the gift demanded than it was granted.

When the skin was brought to her, the frightened princess burst into tears. But her fairy godmother told her that an honest heart need never fear. She advised the girl to pretend to agree to marry the king, but to take her first chance to flee, alone and in disguise, to some distant land.

The fairy godmother said, "Here is my wand. If you hold it in your hand, all your dresses and jewels will follow you in this chest. It will be hidden underground, but when you want to open it, all you need do is strike the ground with the wand. You can wear the donkey's skin as your disguise. No one will believe that anything beautiful could be hidden under that foul thing.''

So the princess crept away in the donkey skin, while the king prepared the wedding feast. He was furious when he learned she was gone, but it was no use; she could not be found.

Meanwhile, the princess continued on her way, her face smeared with filth, begging from passersby and trying to find a job as a servant. But even the poorest households didn't want to take in such an ugly, dirty creature. So she went far, far away and farther still, until finally she came to a small farm where the farmer's wife needed a wench to wash the rags and clean out the pigsty.

They put her in the corner of the kitchen, where all the menservants, insolent vermin that they were, teased and cheeked and pestered her, harassing her at every turn and making her the butt of all their coarse jokes.

Sunday was her only breathing space, when she could go to her little room, wash off all the filth, open the chest, and take out her beautiful dresses. Sometimes she put on the dress that glowed like the moon, sometimes the one that flashed like the sun, and sometimes the one that all the glory of the skies couldn't match. She loved to look at herself in the mirror, so young and pink and a hundred times prettier than anyone else. This sweet pleasure kept her going for another week of drudgery.

Now on this farm was the aviary of a great and powerful king, where he kept his peacocks and other rare birds. One day the king's son stopped by on his way back from the hunt. As soon as she saw him, Donkeyskin knew that beneath her filth and rags there still beat the heart of a princess. "How bold and handsome he is," she said to herself. "The girl who gets him will be lucky. If he gave me rags I would wear them before any of my beautiful dresses."

As it was a Sunday, it happened that the prince passed outside Donkeyskin's door just as she was trying on her dress like the sun, and, on an impulse, he looked through the keyhole. His heart was ravished by the sight; he could barely breathe. It wasn't just her dress, but the beauty of her face, her shapeliness, her youthful freshness, combined with an instinctive grace and air of wisdom and modesty, that captured him. The beauty of her soul overwhelmed his heart.

Three times he nearly broke down the door, but, thinking that he was spying on a goddess, three times he let his arm drop. He went back to the palace in a daze. He sickened, and lost all appetite. He wouldn't go hunting, or see a play, or attend a ball. Everything made him feel ill. Nothing seemed real.

When he asked about the wonderful nymph he had seen, people laughed. "There's no nymph there," they said. "Only ugly Donkeyskin, and she's enough to put anyone off love for life." But the prince could not believe it. He could not forget the girl he had seen through the keyhole.

Meanwhile the queen, his mother, was in despair. She could not find out what was wrong. All he did was groan and cry, and say that the only

thing he wanted was for Donkeyskin to make him a cake with her own hands. The mother didn't know what her son meant. Her servants told her, "Heavens, ma'am, this Donkeyskin is an ugly mole, more ragged than the scruffiest kitchen boy."

"Never mind," said the queen. "We must do what he wants." His mother loved him so much she would have given him gold to eat, if that was what he fancied.

So Donkeyskin took some flour, sugar, butter, and fresh eggs, and shut herself up in her room so that she could make her cake properly. She cleaned her hands, arms, and face; quickly laced on a silver bodice so she could work with dignity; and set to.

Whether she was hurrying too much as she worked, or whether she did it on purpose because she had noticed the prince spying on her, we shall never know, but Donkeyskin dropped one of her beautiful rings from her finger into the mixture, and baked it in the cake.

The cake was delicious, and the prince ate it so greedily he nearly swallowed the ring too. When he saw the wonderful emerald on it, and the narrow band of gold in the shape of the finger that wore it, his heart was filled with joy. He put the ring under his pillow.

But still the prince did not recover. In fact he grew worse every day. He grew thinner and thinner, until at last the doctors said there was no use in treating him; as the prince was lovesick, the only cure was marriage. The prince agreed, then surprised them all by producing the ring and saying, "I will only marry the girl whose finger fits this ring."

There was no shortage of applicants. First came the princesses, then the marchionesses and duchesses, but though their fingers were delicate, they were still too thick to pass through the ring. Countesses and baronesses offered their hands one by one, but offered in vain.

Next came the working girls, whose slim and pretty fingers sometimes seemed to fit the ring, but it was always just too small. And finally came the water-carriers and turkey-keepers and all the small fry, whose reddened and blackened paws and thick, pudgy fingers had no chance at all of passing through the prince's ring.

At last the only girl left was Donkeyskin, "And no one can imagine heaven has destined her to be our queen," as everyone said. But the prince asked, "Why not? Have her brought here." Everyone thought this a great joke, and when Donkeyskin arrived, they laughed and jeered at her.

When, from underneath the pelt, Donkeyskin reached out a tiny hand of ivory tinged with purple and slipped a finger into the ring, which fitted her exactly, the whole court gasped in amazement.

They wanted to take her to the king, but she asked leave first to go and put on another dress. They were all prepared to laugh again at Donkeyskin's dress, but when she appeared in her wonderful dress like the sky, all the great ladies of the court suddenly seemed faded and plain. To look at her was both a pleasure and a pain, she was so beautiful, with her lovely blond hair, her soft blue eyes that flashed with inner majesty, and her delicate waist that you could encircle with your two hands.

The king and queen were as happy as the prince to have found such a delightful daughter-in-law, and the wedding was arranged without delay. Guests came from all four corners of the world, and of them all the most welcome was the bride's own father, who had long since recovered from his mad passion and was overjoyed to see his dear daughter once again. The prince, in turn, wasn't displeased to discover his father-in-law was such a powerful king.

The last to come was the fairy godmother, who entertained all the guests with the whole story, and so brought Donkeyskin's extraordinary tale to its end.

MORAL

It's better to suffer than to do wrong;
Sometimes suffering makes you strong.

ANOTHER MORAL

When we are in the grip of passion,
Common sense goes out of fashion.
In love, we'll squander all our treasure,
If it suits our sweetheart's pleasure.

THE FOOLISH WISHES

IF YOU WEREN'T so sensible, I would think twice before telling you such a mad, strange story as I'm about to inflict on you. It's about a sausage. Yes, a sausage. "Ugh!" you might say. But wait a minute. You might like it. I think you will.

There was once a poor woodcutter who was so tired of his miserable life that he wanted to die. He was so sad, he felt that in the whole time he had been in the world cruel heaven had never once fulfilled a single one of his wishes.

One day he was in the woods, grumbling and complaining. Suddenly Jupiter appeared to him, thunderbolt in hand. You can scarcely begin to describe how frightened the man was. "I don't want anything," he said, flinging himself to the ground. "No wishes, no thunder, my lord, let's stay as we are."

"Do not be afraid," said Jupiter. "I have come in response to your complaint, to show you how you wrong me. So listen. I make you this promise — I, the lord of the world — that I will fulfill in their entirety the first three wishes that you make, whatever they might be, whatever may make you happy, whatever your heart desires. And as your happiness depends on these three wishes, think carefully before you make them."

With these words, Jupiter ascended into the skies once more, and the merry woodcutter lifted his bundle onto his back and set off for home. Never had his burden seemed less heavy. As he trotted along, he said, "I mustn't be rash about this. I must get my wife's advice." As he entered his rush-roofed home, he called, "Well now, Fanchon, my dear, let's build a large fire. From now on, we're rich. We've just got to make the wishes." And he told his wife all that had happened.

When she heard the story, his wife soon made a thousand plans, but she too thought they shouldn't be rash. "Blaise, my dear," she said to her husband, "let's not spoil anything by our impatience. We must weigh every-thing carefully between us. Let's put the first wish off until tomorrow, and sleep on it."

"Good idea," said Blaise. "Now, fetch me some wine from behind that wood-pile." When she came back, he drank, and as he relaxed peacefully by the fire, he said, "It's such a good fire, I only wish we had a sausage to fry on it." Scarcely were the words out of his mouth when his wife was astonished to see a very large sausage snaking toward her from the fireplace.

She let out a yell. Realizing that this was the result of her silly husband's stupid wish, she screeched at him in spite and fury. There wasn't any bad name she didn't call him.

"When we could have had an empire," she said, "gold, pearls, rubies, diamonds, beautiful clothes, did it have to be a sausage?"

"Well, I was wrong," he admitted. "I made a poor choice. I made a huge mistake, but I will do better next time."

"Yes, yes," she said, "I'll believe that when I see it. To make a wish like that, you have to be a donkey."

The husband was so angry he thought about wishing to be a widower (and, between you and me, it wasn't such a bad idea). "Men are born to suffer," he said. "A curse on the sausage, and a curse on it again. I wish to God, you old goat, that you had it stuck on the end of your nose!"

No sooner had the wish left his lips than the sausage attached itself to the end of the furious wife's nose. This unexpected wonder drove her wild. She was a pretty woman, and, to tell the truth, her new ornament didn't suit her. And apart from that, it dangled in front of her face and blocked up her mouth so she couldn't speak properly, which might have been an advantage from her husband's point of view, but not from hers.

The woodcutter said to himself, "I could get myself out of all this miserable trouble by using the wish I have left to make myself king in one bound. There's nothing to equal the grandeur of a sovereign. But then there's my wife. How she would suffer as queen, sitting on her throne with a sausage on her nose. I must ask her what she thinks."

He
asked her,
"Would you
rather be a great queen,
and keep that horrible
nose, or remain a woodcutter's
wife, with the nose you had before?"

She thought it over carefully. She knew what a royal throne is worth, and that a crowned head always has a handsome nose. But nothing is more powerful than the desire to be attractive, and she preferred to keep her peasant cap than to be queen and be ugly.

So the woodcutter's condition did not change. He did not become a potentate. He did not fill his purse with gold. His one last wish he used to make his wife happy by giving her back her pretty nose, and he was pleased to do it.

MORAL

To make a wish you first must see
Exactly what your wish is worth;
Or else you'll squander carelessly
The common gifts of human birth.

ABOUT THE STORIES

CHARLES PERRAULT

Charles Perrault was born in Paris on 12 January 1628, and died on 16 May 1703, aged seventy-five. He was the son of Pierre Perrault, a barrister. After graduating as a lawyer at Orléans in 1651, he became clerk to his brother, Pierre, the Receiver General of Paris. Louis XIV's powerful Controller General of Finance, Jean Baptiste Colbert, appointed him to a civil service post overseeing the building of royal palaces such as the Louvre and Versailles, and also employed him as his adviser on artistic matters. In 1672 he married Marie Guidon, and they had three sons and a daughter.

In 1671 Perrault was elected to the prestigious Académie française, where he indulged his taste for literature and enjoyed a celebrated battle of wits with the poet Boileau. After Colbert's death in 1687, Perrault retired to devote himself to writing. In 1691 he published a verse tale in the manner of La Fontaine, "Patient Griselda," dedicated to "Mademoiselle," Elisabeth Charlotte d'Orléans, niece of Louis XIV. "The Foolish Wishes" followed in 1693, and "Donkeyskin" in 1694, drawing from his enemy Boileau the comment that the ass's skin was an appropriate garment for the tale's author. In the same year, all three tales appeared in the *Recueil de pièces curieuses et nouvelles*, published by Moetjens in The Hague, and also in book form.

In February 1696, the first of the eight prose tales, "The Sleeping Beauty," was published in the *Mercure galant*, and subsequently in volume V, part 2, of the *Recueil*. In the following year, Moetjens printed in volume V, part 4, of the *Recueil* the tales of "Little Red Riding Hood," "Bluebeard," "Puss-in-Boots," "The Fairies," "Cinderella," "Tufty Ricky," and "Hop o' My Thumb." The eight tales were then published in Paris by Claude Barbin as *Histoires ou contes du tems passé*; above the frontispiece was an alternative title, *Contes de ma mère l'Oye*, "Tales of Mother Goose."

None of the journal printings had attributed authorship of the tales, and when they appeared in book form Perrault's name was not associated with them. Instead, the introductory dedication to Mademoiselle was signed "P. Darmancour," the name assumed by Perrault's third son, Pierre. This has caused a confusion about the stories' authorship that remains to this day. All the relevant evidence has been marshalled by Jacques Barchilon in his edition of the "dedication manuscript" dated 1695 that was presented to Mademoiselle and is now in the Pierpont Morgan Library, New York. This manuscript contains five of the tales: "The Sleeping Beauty," "Little Red Riding Hood," "Bluebeard," "Puss-in-Boots," and "The Fairies." Pierre would at that time have been aged sixteen or seventeen.

Writing out fairy tales seems an unlikely occupation for a youth of the time, especially one who later showed no literary leanings, and it seems fairly certain that Charles Perrault himself wrote the tales. He had earlier shown a keen interest in the fairy tale, and he had already published the three verse retellings of popular tales. The polished and confident style of the tales is that of a mature writer. Perrault may well have felt it beneath his dignity to have his name too closely associated with lowly peasant tales, especially after Boileau's caustic reception of "Donkeyskin."

Those who knew Perrault seem to have had little doubt of his authorship. Although the unauthorized Amsterdam editions of the tales that soon appeared credited them to "the son of M. Perrault," after his death they changed to, "by M. Perrault." It may be that Perrault learned the tales via Pierre, who may have heard them from a nurse or servant; we shall never know.

Whatever the provenance of the tales, they, and not any of his more earnest and scholarly literary works, were to make Charles Perrault, in the words of Andrew Lang, "immortal by a kind of accident."

TRANSLATING PERRAULT

The first English translation of Perrault's fairy tales was made by Robert Samber in 1729; luckily, it was an excellent attempt at rendering Perrault's terse, vivid prose, giving all subsequent retellings and reworkings a sound basis in the original. Many of Samber's versions have been reprinted by the Opies in their collection *The Classic Fairy Tales*.

Translating Perrault anew, we have gone back to the French text, using as the basis of our work Andrew Lang's 1888 edition, which was in turn taken from the orginal Paris edition of 1697. We have also consulted a 1698 reprint in the British Library, Gilbert Rouger's 1967 critical edition, and Jacques Barchilon's edition of the 1695 manuscript of five stories in the Pierpont Morgan Library.

It is hard to convey in English translation the splendid brevity of Perrault's prose. His distinctive wit and elegance are based in succinctness and economy. Many retellings of stories such as "Cinderella" replace this asperity with a winsome, sentimental air that is entirely absent from the original text.

Although we have worked from a strict literal translation of

Perrault's French, we have allowed ourselves some leeway to produce a modern English version that is as readable and expressive as possible. We have, in particular, exercised a good deal of freedom in translating the sentimental-cum-cynical rhymed "morals" that Perrault appended to the stories, though the basic sense is his.

In the case of the three verse tales, "Patient Griselda," "Donkeyskin," and "The Foolish Wishes," we offer a shortened prose paraphrase in the style of the prose tales rather than a word-for-word translation.

THE SLEEPING BEAUTY
La belle au bois dormant

"The Sleeping Beauty in the Wood," to give the tale its full title, is one of the most popular of all fairy tales, but oddly enough it is quite rare in oral tradition. Geneviève Massignon does include in her *Folktales of France* a story recorded from a farmer in Angoumois in 1959, in which the princess lies asleep in a castle guarded by a monster with seven heads, which the prince must cut off all at once, or else new heads will grow.

Most oral versions seem to derive from one or another of the literary texts. The Grimms' "Little Briar-Rose," for instance, recorded from a woman of French origin, is clearly based on Perrault's tale. Perrault's sources in turn lie in the anonymous medieval romance *Perceforest*, and the story of "Sun, Moon, and Talia" in the *Pentamerone* of Basile (1643-46).

Stories no. 16 in Pino-Saavedra, *Folktales of Chile*, and no. 14 in Roberts, *South from Hell-fer-Sartin*, show how the tale survived the journey to the New World. The nearest to a "Sleeping Beauty" tale in English tradition is the story "Lousy Jack and His Eleven Brothers" told to T. W. Thompson by the gypsy master storyteller Taimi Boswell, and printed in Philip, *The Penguin Book of English Folktales*. Taimi's tale is a skit on a much longer story, "The Castle o' the Golden Phoenix, the Bottle o' Eversee Water and the Three Sleeping Beauties," which apparently took six hours to tell, and which went unrecorded. In "Lousy Jack," the hero makes his way into the enchanted castle to wake the princess by accident; he makes his way through the thorns not out of bravery and a sense of adventure but because "being such a lousy fella he liked de scratching he got, and kept on pushing his way through 'em on dat account, just for de sake 'n de scratching."

LITTLE RED RIDING HOOD
Le Petit Chaperon Rouge

In the Grimms' "Little Red-Cap," a story collected from a narrator of French Huguenot stock and clearly derived from Perrault, a huntsman appears at the end to cut Little Red-Cap and her grandmother alive from the stomach of the wolf. Many retellers of Perrault's tale have followed this ending, or elaborated even further: Iona and Peter Opie note, "In Madame de Chatelain's *Merry Tales for Little Folk*, 1868, on the other hand, the wolf was just about to spring at Little Red Ridinghood when a wasp stung his nostril, which gave a signal to a tomtit, which warned a huntsman, who let fly an arrow 'that struck the wolf right through the ear and killed him on the spot.' "

Delarue and Tenèze list thirty-five French variants, of which two are taken directly from Perrault, a dozen have mixed oral and literary roots, and twenty owe nothing to the literary tale. In these the heroine does not even have her familiar name, she is just "a little girl." All of these oral versions include the "cruel and primitive" motif of the girl being made to eat her grandmother's flesh and drink her blood, which was no doubt deliberately omitted by Perrault. Most versions end, like Perrault's, with the dramatic dialogue between the girl and the disguised wolf, at the end of which the girl is devoured. In some, she escapes, usually by telling the wolf she has to step outside to answer a call of nature; the wolf ties a string to her leg, but she unties this and fastens it to a tree while she makes her escape.

Further French versions readily available include "The Grandmother" in Delarue, *French Folktales*, and "Boudin-Boudine" in Massignon, *Folktales of France*. Although essentially a European story, versions collected in the United States include "The Bear Ate Them Up" in Randolph, *Sticks in the Knapsack*, and "The Gunny Wolf" in Botkin, *A Treasury of American Folklore*. Carrière's *Tales from the French Folk-Lore of Mississippi* contains a French-American variant told by Joseph Ben Coleman, "L'P'tsit Jupon Rouge et pis l'P'tsit Chapeau Rouge," in which a boy and a girl are sent with a pot of butter to their grandmother. The wolf eats the grandmother and the children, but their father rescues them and cuts all three alive from the stomach of the wolf.

Although, or because, it has traditionally been told to children as a "frightener," "Little Red Riding Hood" has always been popular with young audiences, but never more so than with Charles Dickens, who recorded, "She was my first love. I felt that if I could have married Little Red Riding-Hood, I should have known perfect bliss. But, it was not to be."

BLUEBEARD
La Barbe Bleüe

This tale, with its disturbing and violent view of male-female relations, has always exercised a curious attraction-cum-repulsion for readers and listeners, producing an uneasy feeling which has been imaginatively explored in Angela Carter's adult variations on the theme, *The Bloody Chamber*.

It is a popular tale type in France, where thirty-nine French analogues of Perrault's "Bluebeard" have been collected. Usually in these the bride's vital few minutes are won when she goes up to her chamber to put on her wedding dress in which to be killed. Also, she usually alerts her brothers or parents by means of an animal messenger such as a little dog or a bird. Another French version, "The White Dove," can be found in Delarue, *French Folktales*.

France also has versions of two variant forms of the tale: the one familiar from the Grimms' "Fitcher's Bird," and a Christianized form particular to central France. Britain, too, has a local variant of the international type, best known as "The Story of Mr. Fox"; this and six related versions can be found in Philip, *The Penguin Book of English Folktales*. A number of tellings have also been noted in the United States, among them "The Bloody House" in Roberts, *South from Hell-fer-Sartin*.

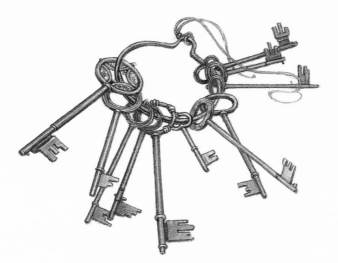

PUSS-IN-BOOTS

Le maistre chat, ou le chat botté

The earliest printed "Puss-in-Boots" tale is "Constantino For-
tunato" in the *Piacevoli notti (Facetious Nights)* of Straparola
(1550-53). Of fifteen recorded French versions, eleven follow
Perrault in having a cat as the hero's helper; one such is "Puss-
in-Boots" in Massignon, *Folktales of France*. The other four, such
as "The Gilded Fox" in Delarue, *French Folktales*, feature a fox, a

creature which also appears in this role in many other countries. Carrière's collection of French folktales collected from Joseph Ben Coleman in Old Mines, Missouri, in the 1930s includes "L'chat botté," which is very close to Perrault, even to the name the Marquis of Carabas, showing how persistent literary influences can be in an oral tradition. In the case of the Old Mines community, all the families living there in the 1930s were descended from Creoles who had settled in the district by 1820, and whose ancestors had founded French villages in Illinois between 1699 and 1760.

THE FAIRIES
Les fées

Forty French versions have been recorded of this widely spread international folktale, known to scholars as "The Spinning-Women by the Spring," or, "The Kind and Unkind Girls." In fact a heavily embroidered French version, "Les enchantemens de l'eloquence ou les effets de la douceur," by Mlle. L'Heritier de Villaudon, was published in 1695, prior to Perrault's tale. Mlle. L'Heritier was a friend and relative of Perrault, and she may have learned the tale from him, or, as some think, he may have borrowed the plot from her. In 1695 Perrault described the typical fairy tale as one in which the fairies reward a civil young woman with the gift of uttering a diamond or a pearl with every word, and a rude one with the curse of spewing out a frog or a serpent. In the manuscript version of 1695, the sisters in "The Fairies" are stepsisters, the younger girl being the daughter of the father's first wife; Perrault apparently altered this when he decided to include the story of "Cinderella" in his collection, to avoid having two such similar openings.

Marie Campbell's *Tales from the Cloud Walking Country* contains a number of American variations on this tale type. In English variants, the rewards are typically given not by fairies but by three heads in a well. In George Peele's fairytale play of 1595, *The Old Wives' Tale*, the heads memorably sing:

138

Gently dip, but not too deep,

For fear thou make the golden beard to weep.

Fair maid, white and red,

Comb me smooth, and stroke my head;

And every hair, a sheave shall be,

And every sheave a golden tree.

The tale type has been thoroughly studied by Warren E. Roberts in *The Tale of the Kind and Unkind Girls*.

CINDERELLA

Cendrillon, ou la petite pantoufle de verre

"Cinderella" must be the most famous fairy tale in the world, and, in its various oral forms, one of the most widely spread. It is not, however, known worldwide, as is sometimes stated; the tale is not native to Africa, Australasia, or the Americas, though it has become localized in all those places. "Cinderella" has also been one of the most intensively studied of all folktales, with at least four books exclusively devoted to it. In all this welter of oral versions (including more than a hundred French variants of the stories in "the Cinderella cycle" and many hundreds from all over Europe and Asia), it is easy to lose track of what is special about Perrault's particular version. In fact Perrault's telling, with its courtly air and its thrilling transformations, has stamped his personality indelibly on the tale. The Scottish writer David Toulmin, searching for a way to describe the wonder and strangeness of a rich, unexplored house, need only write, "It was all so Cinderella," to be immediately understood.

"Cinderella," like Perrault's other tales, became widely known in Britain in the eighteenth and nineteenth centuries by means of the cheap paper editions known as chapbooks. It was no doubt from one of these that the story became known in Helpstone, Northamptonshire, the home village of the peasant poet John Clare. In his *Shepherd's Calendar* (1827) he remembers with affection,

> The tale of Cinderella told
> The winter thro and never old
> The faireys favourite and friend
> Who made her happy in the end
> The pumpkin that at her approach
> Was turned into a golden coach
> The rats that faireys magic knew
> And instantly to horses grew
> And coachmen ready at her call
> To drive her to the prince's ball
> With fur-changd jackets silver lind
> And tails hung neath their hats behind
> Where soon as met the princes sight
> She made his heart ach all the night
> The golden glove wi fingers small
> She lost while dancing in the hall
> That was on every finger tryd
> And fitted hers and none beside
> When cinderella soon as seen
> Was woo'd and won and made a queen.

Although village storytelling has exchanged Perrault's glass slipper for a golden glove, this is clearly still his story: the rat coachmen and pumpkin coach were Perrault's invention.

Perrault's "fairy godmother" is a more literary way of approaching one of the key elements of oral tellings: the help that Cinderella receives from the spirit of her dead mother, often in animal form. In the oral "Cinderella" in Massignon, *Folktales of France*, recorded in 1961 from a seventy-three-year-old peasant woman, Mme. Joly, at Saint-Maurice des Lions, Charente, the help comes from "the Holy Virgin."

The first recorded Cinderella story was written down in China in the 9th century A.D. Translated by Arthur Waley as "Yeh-hsien," it can be found in Philip, *The Cinderella Story*.

TUFTY RICKY
Riquet à la Houppe

"Tufty Ricky" is the only one of Perrault's tales that has no obvious claim to being a "tale of Mother Goose." It seems instead to be a literary imitation of a traditional tale, based on elements of a fairy-tale novel published by Mlle. Bernard in 1696, just a few months before Perrault's own book went to press. Interestingly, it has always been the least popular of Perrault's stories, though gauged against other literary fairy tales it is a decided success. Perrault's stories were the most important product of a fashionable craze for the fairy tale that started in the 1670s, when the ladies and dandies of the French court began to tell peasant tales for amusement in much the same way as they dressed up as shepherds and shepherdesses at their balls. In the years that followed the publication of Perrault's simply told tales, a flood of ever more elaborate and fanciful fairy tales was published, culminating in an immense library of fairy tales, known as the *Cabinet des fées*, which ran to forty-one volumes. The most prominent authors in this literary movement, which produced very little of lasting worth, include Mme. Leprince de Beaumont, author of ''Beauty and the Beast,'' Mme. d'Aulnoy, author of ''The Yellow Dwarf,'' and the Comte de Caylus, four of whose stories survive in Andrew Lang's *Green Fairy Book*.

HOP O' MY THUMB
Le petit Pouçet

Eighty-two versions of this story have been collected from oral storytellers in France, such as "Jean and Jeanette" in Massignon, *Folktales of France*. Such popularity for this story, with its grim evidence of the deadening effect of poverty and hunger on the emotions, tells its own tale. The motif of the children being abandoned in the forest is most familiar from the Grimms' "Hansel and Gretel." It is not always present in tales of this type, known to folklorists as "The Children and the Ogre." In the Gaelic story of "Maol a Chliobain" (in Philip, *The Penguin Book of Scottish Folktales*), three daughters leave home. Their mother gives them food for their journey, with the choice of "the big half and my curse or the little half and my blessing." The two older sisters choose the big half; the youngest takes the little half and the blessing. On their journey, the two older sisters try to lose the youngest, by, for instance, tying her to a rock. But each time, "her mother's blessing came and freed her." Once they get to the giant's house, the story falls into the lines of Perrault's, though without such literary elements as the seven-league boots; Maol a Chliobain escapes the giant by plucking a hair from her head and using it as a bridge across a river, which she can run across but he cannot.

The hero of Perrault's tale does not, despite his name, seem to be particularly small, other than being, like Maol a Chliobain, the youngest of the family. His name seems to have crept into the tale by accident from some real "Thumbling" story such as the English "Tom Thumb." Perrault's tale is sometimes, misleadingly, translated as "Tom Thumb," but the two stories are in fact quite different. The point about Tom Thumb is that he really is no bigger than a thumb, whereas Hop o' My Thumb seems a normal-sized boy.

One of the earliest Cinderella stories, Mme. d'Aulnoy's "Finette-Cendron," blends this tale type with Cinderella; an oral version of this, "Belle Finette," was collected by Carrière in Missouri in the 1930s, and printed in his *Tales from the French Folk-Lore of Missouri*.

PATIENT GRISELDA

Griselidis

"Patient Griselda" was Perrault's first attempt at versifying a popular tale in the manner of La Fontaine, and was published, with a dedication to Mademoiselle, in 1691. It is a rather long-winded poem, and in making this prose version we have abbreviated where possible.

The story of Patient Griselda and her triumph through submissiveness is scarcely in tune with modern thinking, and the temptation to recommend a course of assertiveness training is hard to resist. Even Perrault seems to have been aware that few readers would genuinely admire Griselda's self-abasement, but would interpret it as lack of spirit rather than patience and inner strength. Nevertheless the story has a distinguished literary history. Perrault almost certainly found it in the *Decameron* of Boccaccio (day 10, tale 10), but it also provided Chaucer with his "Clerk's Tale" in *The Canterbury Tales*.

DONKEYSKIN

Peau d'Asne

"Donkeyskin," which Perrault published in verse form, is actually a close variant of "Cinderella." The parallel between the ring that will fit only Donkeyskin and the slipper that will fit only Cinderella would be even more obvious if the prince in this story saw Donkeyskin three times, once in each of her beautiful dresses. Such meetings can take place at a ball or party lasting three nights, or, in Catholic countries, on three successive Sundays, at mass. The motif of the king wishing to marry his daughter is very common; another variant is the "King Lear" opening in which the father asks his daughters how much they love him, and the youngest answers, "As much as fresh meat loves salt." She is banished, and her story follows that of Donkeyskin. Her father is invited to her wedding feast, when all the meat is served unsalted and tasteless, and he realizes that she did love him after all.

Thirty-nine versions of this widespread tale, known to scholars as "The Dress of Gold, of Silver, and of Stars," have been recorded in France, including "The She-Donkey's Skin" in Massignon, *Folktales of France*.

THE FOOLISH WISHES
Les souhaits ridicules

Perrault may have heard the story of "The Foolish Wishes" from oral tradition, but it also has a long literary history, stretching back to the *Panchatantra* and the ninth-century *Book of Sindibâd*. Variants of the story are common in the fabliaux and jestbooks of the Middle Ages, and there is a good version, evidently based on an English original, among the twelfth-century poems of Marie de France.

Stories about the ridiculous waste of wishes are sometimes obscene (as in the five-hundred-and-second of the *Thousand and One Nights*) or scatological (as in the version from Maine in Richard Dorson's *Buying the Wind*, p. 83), but the homely version known to Perrault, in which the couple wish first for a sausage, then that the sausage was on the nose of one of them, and then that it was off again, is the most widespread. Thomas Sternberg's *Dialect and Folk-Lore of Northamptonshire* (1851) preserves a rudimentary English version, expanded by Alfred Nutt in Joseph Jacobs's *More English Fairy Tales*.

While the wasted-wishes theme does make a satisfactory story by itself, it is often associated with stories of the wanderings on earth of Christ and St. Peter. Disguised as ordinary men, they are welcomed in one house and spurned in another. In both cases they grant three wishes, which the hospitable peasant uses wisely, but the inhospitable one foolishly. The best-known version of this fuller tale is the Grimms' "The Poor Man and the Rich Man."

No one in a folktale ever seems to think of wishing for more wishes, though no doubt if they did so out of greed it would rebound on them in some dreadful and unforeseen way.

FURTHER READING

The Fairy Tales of Perrault

Perrault, Charles. *Histoires ou contes du tems passé. Avec des moralitez.* Paris: Claude Barbin, 1698 (1st ed., 1697).

———. *Perrault's Popular Tales.* Edited from the original editions, with introduction, etc. by Andrew Lang. Oxford: Clarendon Press, 1888.

———. *Perrault's Tales of Mother Goose.* The dedication manuscript of 1695 reproduced in collotype facsimile with introduction and critical text by Jacques Barchilon. New York: The Pierpont Morgan Library, 1956.

———. *Perrault's Complete Fairy Tales.* Translated from the French by A. E. Johnson and others. New York: Dodd, Mead & Company, 1961; London: Constable, 1962.

———. *Contes.* Textes établis, avec introduction, sommaire biographique, bibliographie, notices, relevé de variantes, notes et glossaire par Gilbert Rouger. Paris: Classiques Garnier, 1967.

———. *The Fairy Tales of Charles Perrault.* Translated by Angela Carter. London: Victor Gollancz, 1977.

The French Folktale

Carrière, Joseph Médard. *Tales from the French Folk-Lore of Missouri.* Evanston & Chicago: Northwestern University, 1937.

Delarue, Paul. *The Borzoi Book of French Folk Tales.* Translated by Austin E. Fife. New York: Alfred A. Knopf, 1956.

Delarue, Paul, and Tenèze, Marie-Louise. *Le conte populaire français*. Volume 1, Paris: Editions Erasme, 1957. Volumes 2 & 3, Paris: Editions Maisonneuve et Larose, 1964 & 1976.

Massignon, Geneviève. *Folktales of France*. Chicago & London: The University of Chicago Press, 1968.

Thomas, Rosemary Hyde. *It's Good to Tell You: French Folktales from Missouri*. Columbia & London: University of Missouri Press, 1981.

The International Folktale

Aarne, Antti. *The Types of the Folktale*. Translated and enlarged by Stith Thompson. 2nd revision, Folklore Fellows Communications No. 184. Helsinki: Suomalainen Tiedeakatemia, Academia Scientiarum Fennica, 1961.

Ashliman, D. L. *A Guide to Folktales in the English Language, Based on the Aarne-Thompson Classification System*. Bibliographies and Indexes in World Literature No. 11. New York; Westport, Connecticut; London: Greenwood Press, 1987.

Basile, Giambattista. *The Pentamerone*. Translated from the Italian of Benedetto Croce, edited with a preface, notes and appendixes by N. M. Penzer. 2 vols. London: John Lane the Bodley Head Ltd, 1932.

Baughman, Ernest W. *Type and Motif Index of the Folk-Tales of England and North America*. Indiana University Folklore Series No. 20. The Hague: Mouton & Co., 1966.

Boccaccio, Giovanni. *The Decameron*. Translated and with an introduction by G.H. McWilliam. New York: Penguin Books, 1972.

Bolte, J., and Polívka, G. *Anmerkungen zu den kinder –u. hausmärchen der brüder Grimm*. 5 vols. Leipzig: Dieterich'sche Verlagsbuchhandlung, 1913-32.

Botkin, B. A. *A Treasury of American Folklore: Stories, Ballads, and Traditions of the People*. New York: Crown Publishers, 1944.

Briggs, Katharine M. *A Dictionary of British Folk-Tales in the English Language, Incorporating the F. J. Norton Collection*. 4 vols. London: Routledge & Kegan Paul, 1970-1.

Campbell, Marie. *Tales from the Cloud Walking Country*. Bloomington: Indiana University Press, 1958.

Carter, Angela. *The Bloody Chamber*. London: Victor Gollancz; New York: Harper & Row, 1979.

Clare, John. *The Shepherd's Calendar*. Edited by Eric Robinson and Geoffrey Summerfield. London: Oxford University Press, 1964.

Dorson, Richard M. *Buying the Wind: Regional Folklore in the United States*. Chicago & London: The University of Chicago Press, 1964.

Dundes, Alan. *Cinderella: A Case Book*. New York & London: Garland Publishing, 1983.

Grimm, Jacob, and Grimm, Wilhelm. *Grimm's Tales for Young and Old*. Translated by Ralph Manheim. New York: Anchor Press/Doubleday, 1977; London: Victor Gollancz, 1978.

——. *The Complete Fairy Tales of the Brothers Grimm*. Translated by Jack Zipes. New York: Bantam, 1987.

Jacobs, Joseph. *English Fairy Tales, being the two collections, English Fairy Tales and More English Fairy Tales*. London: The Bodley Head, 1968.

Lang, Andrew. *Green Fairy Book*. Edited by Brian Alderson. London: Kestrel Books; New York: The Viking Press, 1978.

Opie, Iona, and Opie, Peter. *The Classic Fairy Tales*. London: Oxford University Press, 1974.

Mathers, Powys. *The Book of the Thousand Nights and One Night*. Rendered into English from the literal and complete French translation of Dr. J. C. Mardrus. 4 vols. London: George Routledge & Sons, 1937.

Philip, Neil. *The Cinderella Story*. London: Penguin Books, 1989.

——. *The Penguin Book of English Folktales*. London: Penguin Books, 1992.

——. *The Penguin Book of Scottish Folktales*. London: Penguin Books, 1993.

Pino-Saavedra, Yolando. *Folktales of Chile*. Chicago: The University of Chicago Press, 1967; London: Routledge & Kegan Paul, 1968.

Randolph, Vance. *Sticks in the Knapsack and other Ozark Folktales*. New York: Columbia University Press, 1958.

Roberts, Leonard. *South from Hell-fer-Sartin: Kentucky Mountain Folk Tales*. Lexington: University of Kentucky Press, 1955.

Roberts, Warren E. *The Tale of the Kind and Unkind Girls*. Berlin: Walter de Gruyter and Company, 1958.

Rooth, Anna Birgitta. *The Cinderella Cycle*. Lund: C. W. K. Gleerup, 1951.

Straparola, Giovanni Francesco. *The Facetious Nights*. 4 vols. London: Privately Printed for the Society of Bibliophiles, 1901.

Thompson, Stith. *The Folktale*. New York: Holt, Rinehart & Winston, 1946; reprinted Berkeley, Los Angeles, London: University of California Press, 1977.

Zipes, Jack. *The Trials and Tribulations of Little Red Riding Hood*. South Hadley: Bergin & Garvey, 1983.